A Love Forged in Battle

Wilma Ranclaud

Contents

Chapter 1

England, 1066, Senlac Hill

The massive black beast beneath him snickered uneasily, shaking its sleek head as the stallion paced sideways, its large hooves treading the muggy earth.

Fallon Macaulay tightened his hold around the reins to steady Thor, cursing the animal for his uncanny sensibilities to impending danger.

Beneath his steel helmet, he cast a fleeting glance to the lingering gray sky, noting a thickness of clouds brimming with what appeared to soon be a downfall of heavy rain accompanied with brisk winds.

He smirked inwardly for the shaded weather was as disagreeable as the current King sitting on the English throne.

Allegedly the crown had been promised to William by his cousin and former King, Edward the Confessor, but upon his deathbed, believed in a form of desperation after having produced no children during his lifetime, Edward had announced Harold Godwinson, brother to Queen Edith, as heir to the throne.

When informed of Harold's coronation, William became furious for an oath between the two had been violated. Harold had once pledged his allegiance to William after being rescued by the Duke when shipwrecked but the day after Edward's death, the crown was claimed by Godwinson and their treaty was broken. William was not to become successor to the English crown.

Fallon slid a glance sideways, studying the man intently to his left. He and a thousand others, equipped in battle armor waited atop a steep slope for one purpose alone; to ensure that William the Duke of Normandy, rightful heir to the English throne, seized his legitimate crown from Godwinson.

William's fierce expression revealed naught but instead implanted a deep crease across his forehead, his brooding countenance as stoic as granite, and a sharp gleam flared with intensity as his dark eyes swept along his army.

The time was nearly at hand. Fallon felt that familiar rush of adrenaline; anticipating a drawn out battle that would undoubtedly leave a monumental spread of fallen men and a certain effect on the English throne.

Harold and his army traveled from York as William had stationed his men in East Sussex, waiting patiently for the enemy.

The chain of warriors arranged on either side of him suddenly tensed in readiness and an abrupt hushed silence fell among them as the hum of a thousand men broadened the rolling hills. As if on queue, Harold appeared, marching his soldiers forward and positioning them atop the hill. Harold Godwinson, a burly man of size with long shaggy hair and an equally thick beard, aligned his men of household troops on either side of him, placing supporting troops at the rear.

William had chosen a different tactic by taking the rear himself with his armored cavalry on each side of him, the infantry placed within the center and a number of archers planted directly front line.

Fallon's eyes swept the crowd of men around him, all painstakingly familiar, much alike kin but there was one face in particular he sought and failed to find.

Where the hell was Curran?

The man at his side shifted and Fallon jarred alert, shifting his attention to William, his liege.

"The time is now, Fallon "The Fury". Do you swear fealty to me and serve me now?" surprisingly William's voice was tranquil, but there was always a moment of quiet before the storm.

Fallon nodded, meeting William's dark, calculating stare. "Aye milord, until I am claimed by death, I shall serve you at best."

And forthwith, the battle commenced as Saxons hurled an unexpected flare of stones across the distance separating them, delivering painful and fatal blows to unsuspecting Normans.

Fallon gritted his teeth at a number of war cries and raised his shield to deflect the heavy pellets.

Along the front line, archers released a flurry of arrows in hopes of weakening the Saxon lines; this same strategy was repeated several times but barely made a mark, there-fore pushing men on foot into battle, creating a remarkable shudder in the ground as the unmistakable sound of steel clashing against steel resonated through the air.

The shrieks and cries of warriors as they wielded and branded their weapons were frighteningly discernible, coat-ing the soggy turf in red as belligerent blows rendered men hapless at the feet of others.

Fallon felt the fury that which he were befittingly entitled, rise to such a minatory degree as men he called kindred fell so quickly, their lives taken abruptly by spears tossed efficiently.

He glanced at William, watching the massacre with little to no emotion displayed, and felt his temper rising ever more.

"The enemy lines have not faltered." He shouted, watching as more Norman soldiers fell to the ground.

Men were slain mercilessly, taken down easily by relentless Saxon attacks. William's army began to diminish as the Saxon line remained firm without as much as a mark.

Fallon grew restless, forced to remain at William's side, having pledged his loyalty to protect his leader at all costs, but the carnage that continued left him feeling maddeningly useless.

Somewhere within that bloodbath, his brother along with several close allies, fought for the same purpose but as his eyes swept repeatedly over the combined armies, Curran and the others were no where to be found.

He gave one last intensifying look to William and extracted his sword, gripping the hilt with iron force as he spewed forth into the madness.

His agility kept him keenly aware of all his angles; he remained close to ensure that William's back was protected as he swept his sword in a full loop, severing a man in two, pausing only a fraction to readjust his grip and bring the blade about to pierce the heart of another.

As he swiveled around, his sword connected sharply with a Saxon blade. He brought his foot upward and shoved at the man's midriff, forcing the warrior backward onto his backside. From his peripheral, Fallon caught a large, familiar stature. He turned just to see Ranulf, ally from youth, stagger on his feet as two Saxon soldiers of similar size advance towards the large warrior.

Fallon released a nasty growl as he gathered his strength and rushed at his enemy. One of the men caught his livid frame charging toward him and turned half-way to intercept his attack. The other Saxon was momentarily distracted by his comrade that it gave Ranulf the opportunity to bring his axe down up the man, the devastating blow severing his head completely from his shoulders.

Fallon ducked just as the edge of the sword whisked above his head, he rolled beneath the Saxon's raised arm and came lithely to his feet turning to plunge his blade deeply into the man's chest.

Ranulf exchanged a brief look of gratitude before turning away and disappearing into the multitude of men.

As the war waged on and time was of no importance, the number of lives given way to Godwinson rapidly grew.

It was then realized that men were fleeing from the left flank, causing a great break in William's line. Fallon straightened and in that moment caught his brother disappearing among those running.

There was a shrill of chaos as the opposing army separated, breaking into fragments to chase after those who had fled.

Fallon hesitated, torn between whether he should stay at William's side or chase after his brother. His instincts warned him to do the latter, knowing full well of Curran's hankering for battle which could very well be his downfall.

Mumbling a stream of curses beneath his breath, and suddenly feeling the weight of his armor, he broke into a run and started towards Thor as the stallion paced fearfully in the midst of the fright, its beady dark eyes recognizing its master as Fallon came forward. Thor obediently stilled as Fallon mounted and whirled the stallion down over the hill.

The cries of men faded into the background as Fallon fastened his fingers tightly around the reins as Thor's hooves pounded into the earth. He felt beads of perspiration gliding smoothly down his back beneath his chain mail and felt the stickiness of blood along his face beneath his helmet. He wanted nothing more in that moment than to bathe the ugliness of war from his body and forget this day, but as hard as he could try, their was no denying his lineage, his purpose in life, he was bred to kill.

Thor carried him further and further away from William and the battle. He was suddenly aware that there was no one, not even the enemy, around him. An outlandish and slightly serene quiet settled around him, enveloping him in a calm that struck him unaware, allowing him a brief moment to savor the solace and dream on a life that was not of bloodshed and war.

The notion was shattered instantaneously at the abrupt cries of men. He realized then how far he had gone from the hill; he now stood in the thick of trees, shadowing around him, concealing any imposing threats that lay in waiting.

With the trees towering above him, dimness immersed, forcing his senses alert as his eyes strained against the foliage. His brows furrowed as a deep inkling warned him that something was amiss.

Suddenly, their was a disturbance in the silence, a slight crack and snap as something leapt out from behind him. Atop Thor, he was at a disadvantage as he attempted to turn in the saddle, only to be struck forcefully upon the head.

Even with the protection of his helmet, it did not prevent the intense crack that unsaddled him. He hit the ground with such force that the air whooshed from his lungs.

He moaned as he attempted to lift his head, his eyes blinking rapidly with the pain as he rolled to his side, his hands fumbling over the loose dirt.

The hairs on the back of his neck stood tall as several pairs of booted feet suddenly appeared, one set in particular kicking his sword from his reach.

He cursed mindlessly as he attempted to get up only to receive a steadfast kick to the ribs. He gasped in pain and choked as he fought to gather a breath in his lungs just as a pair of hands whipped out and jerked the helmet from his head.

Fallon raised his head to look upon his enemy but instantly a boot connected painfully with his face. The jolt jerked him sideways and a shot of blood projected from his mouth.

Another boot merged with his ribs and he felt a blinding pain as this was done continuously. Through the heedless haze of pain, Fallon heard the distinct sound of laughter but the voice to him was vague, the source of the chuckle a mere blur to the side of him.

He felt himself slipping into unconsciousness but not before something sharp was plunged deep into his chest. Fallon buckled against the pain as the dagger was forced deeper into his flesh, emitting a guttural sound from deep within his throat to surface.

Pain washed over him as he struggled to grab hold of the dagger protruding from his chest. Each labored breath brought on a flood of spasms that sent blood gushing forth from its wound. He moaned as his fingers wrapped languidly around the hilt sticking upward from his chest, and with what little strength he could muster, jerked the dagger free. A swift and unexpected faintness seized him, pulling him downward and spiraling into darkness.

Chapter 2

"Alana please, you must make haste!" wailed her distressed cousin. Alana McKenna paused long enough in her pursuit of picking wild berries to cast an exasperated leer at Lynette as her older cousin paced a groove into the ground, her eyes, a cerulean blue, resembling the azure sky, moved warily around the forest engaging them.

"I won't be long now, Nettie, just let me gather a basket full and we'll be on our way. Agatha's husband is still very ill and I must have these berries to finish my elixir."

Lynette heaved a sigh of frustration as she glared at Alana's back as she bent to pluck handfuls of berries from the surrounding thickets. "Alana 'tis rumored that there are Norman soldiers in the area!" she hissed beneath her breath.

"Nettie!"

Lynette snorted impatiently but refrained from saying anything further; knowing full well that once Alana was set on something there was nothing that would deter her from her purpose, especially when it came to tending the ill for she had the ability to heal with her exceptional knowledge of herbs and medicines.

Alana was a patient woman, having learned to master that emotion when dealing with the unwell, but Lynette however was not, especially in such an area rumored to be swarming with the enemy.

There little village was nestled quite comfortably in the midst of a dense wooded region and 'twas said that a colossal army of opposing enemies had battled not far from where they resided and that Norman warriors still roamed the area.

Having personally dealt with the likes of Norman pigs, she was sorely aware of their barbarism and distinguishing nature of cruelty that prompted violence and bloodshed. She had first handedly witnessed such savagery as a child, remembering woefully the massacre left in their aftermath.

'I've gathered enough berries for now." Alana's voice penetrated her thoughts and Lynette quickly dismissed the images that would surely resurface from recognition. She had no desire to think of that day or dwell on the pain kept buried beneath an overwhelming magnitude of hatred.

Cradling her basket of berries, Alana made her way to where their horses grazed beneath a peculiar willowing tree.

"Tis almost dusk." Lynette said with a deal of concern. "There will not be much daylight left to lead us back to the village."

"We'll manage just fine." Alana said reassuringly, sensing her cousin's unease. "I know a surrogate route that we can take that will save us some time."

Lynette mounted her horse; eager to return and Alana followed, taking caution to not overturn her berries that she had worked so diligently to retrieve.

The dirt path they trailed twined the forest, interlacing trees with streams of twilight emitting through the canopy of vegetation. Small woodland creatures scurried at their approach, fleeing to a burrow within the ground or to a suspended branch, well above their reach.

Alana smiled inwardly, delighted in her surroundings as a feeling of contentment came over her. She relished in nature and the sense of liberation. She savored the solitude, the freedom to do as she pleased, collecting herbs, frolicking in the river, all to which she had no one to make demands of her.

She did not waste time thinking on the follies of war, the absurd notion that the land belonged to one man in particular sitting upon a dais. It was absolutely senseless.

The land belonged to no one; as did she.

"Alana!" the warning was issued beneath Lynette's breath as her horse jolted to a stop.

Alana frowned as she glanced at her cousin's frozen expression and followed her eyes to something rather large lying inert along their path.

Straining to see the hindrance that blocked their way, Alana slowly dismounted and set her basket at her feet.

"What are you doing?" Lynette whispered alarmingly.

Alana ignored her cousin as she tentatively started towards the solid shape. As she grew closer, an audible gasp escaped her throat as she realized that the large object was a man.

She paused only a moment before starting forward but a hand on her arm stopped her abruptly. "What do you think you are doing?" Lynette demanding pensively, her azure eyes round with misgiving.

"I have to see."

Lynette sighed heavily and dropped her hand. She followed closely at Alana's back as they inched forward to peer at the man, what she saw made her stiffen instinctively with coldness. "He is a Norman!" she hissed with sudden malice.

.

"You cannot know for certain." Alana studied the man's face, gray and colorless beneath a coating of dried blood, his features intangible beneath the disarray among his face. She was unclear as to his origin but he was unmistakably a warrior due to his immense size. She had never seen a man so enormous. Surely it had taken a number of others to bring down such a giant of a man.

His armor had clearly been stripped and taken from his body. He wore naught but under-clothing and by the mass of blood that drenched his apparel, she was unsure as to his injuries.

"Alana, leave him!"

She turned to see Lynette mounted her expression indifferent to the stranger at her feet. "Nettie, help me."

"He is Norman!" she cried, outraged. "How could you even think to aid such a monster?"

"Whether he is Norman or Saxon he is a man nonetheless and needs our help. I cannot simply abide leaving him like this." She replied assertively.

Lynette snorted with distaste. "As I see it, all men are pigs, especially the likes at your feet. I am sorry cousin; I will not assist you in this."

Alana narrowed her eyes as she exhaled sharply through her nose. "Then will you at least go back to the village and bring me something that I could carry him back in?"

Lynette stiffened instantly with disapproval. "I will certainly not leave you here for his army to find you!"

"Then make haste so that I am not here longer than necessary!"

"Alana, you are making a mistake, he will only return your kindness by killing you the moment he is revived."

Alana lifted her chin defiantly. "I will deal with that if it comes, now please, hurry."

Lynette hesitated but the unyielding gleam in her cousin's eyes prompted her decision. "You do not have your bow and arrow; I cannot leave you here defenseless."

Alana had not considered that and her eyes quickly searched the area for something that belonged to the warrior, mayhap a sword or dagger of some sort.

What she discovered made her heart leap within her chest. Lying at the man's side, just at the tips of his fingers, was an ominous dagger, the serrated blade, particularly crafted to inflict fatal wounds, rested at his side.

She felt her stomach churn with nausea as she stared at the ghastly weapon and prayed silently that whoever had delivered the fatal blow would not return to see the purpose done.

"I will be fine." She whispered more so to herself than to Lynette. "Just hurry."

Lynette nodded her face taut with displeasure but she said nothing more as she steered her horse around Alana and started in a canter back towards the village.

Alana watched until her cousin disappeared down the narrowing path, praying that she would return quickly enough to see the three of them safely back to the village.

She realized than just how alone and defenseless she truly was and cast a longing look at the dagger. The thought of touching it made her ill all of a sudden. If it came to it, she would defend the man at all costs but she would not touch it.

She fell to her knees at his side and peered at his massive chest but she could detect no rise and fall that would indicate that he were alive.

She reached out and gingerly pressed her fingers to his throat. Her heart jumped with amazement for as faint as it were, there was a pulse.

"You're alive." She breathed in astonishment.

Without warning, her wrist was suddenly shackled in a menacing iron grip, the unexpectedness of his deftness wrenched a startled gasp from her throat, and her heart leapt tenfold as Lynette's warning fleetingly crossed her mind. She lifted her head from the hand gripping her own and her gaze connected fearfully with a pair of burning, amber eyes.

Chapter 3

The villagers were not pleased to hear that a Norman warrior was in their midst. She received quite a number of scornful glares and a few accosting words from fellow neighbors.

She was grateful that the cottage she and Lynette shared was somewhat secluded from the village. She had chosen the particular hut specifically for its remoteness from others.

With much convincing, several of the village men grudgingly assisted in carrying the unconscious Norman into her cottage. She noticed as they settled the Norman onto her pallet that he appeared frighteningly paler.

Rowan, a robust youth with a wealth of mahogany hair and eyes the color of onyx, were one of the few men assisting her. An adamant look of disapproval was undeniably etched across his brooding face as he waited patiently for the others to leave the cottage, each muttering words of reproach beneath their breath as they cast meaningful glares at Alana.

"Why do you do this, Alana?" Rowan asked gently, waving a hand towards the warrior.

Alana lifted her chin, "I have the ability to heal him." Rowan shook his head, "Not him, not a Norman."

She sighed miserably as she crossed the straw laden floor to the iron kettle hanging above the hearth. "I do not have to explain my motives to you, Rowan, or to anybody else for that matter."

She felt him come up behind her and she stiffened. She knew Rowan had strong feelings for her but those feelings were not shared. Aye, he was noticeably handsome but her feelings went no further than companionship.

"You do not know what his kind is capable of."

"His kind?" she turned sharply only to collide against him for he stood too close. She gasped, startled by this for she had never been intimidated by Rowan before but something about his demeanor gave her reason to pause. "What do you know of his kind, Rowan? You speak as though he were a loathsome beast. I wonder if they have such poor opinions of us as you do them. As I see it, they have every reason to slander us, because you have the indecency to judge them at first glance."

His hands fell freely to her waist and she jerked beneath his touch. "Don't be a fool, Alana. You're winsome heart will steer you wrong." He leaned close enough until his breath fanned her forehead. "He will skewer you the moment he is able."

"Please leave, Rowan. You are wasting my time."

For a moment he hesitated and then slowly he stepped away, his hands falling to his side. "If you have need of me-" he started, glancing harshly in the corner, "-I shan't be far."

She said nothing and waited until he left the hut. Releasing a deep breath, she turned back to the hearth to prepare a broth.

"Have you gone mad?"

She felt a groan in her throat as she turned to peer at Lynette seething in the door way. "It would appear that I have."

"I won't stay here with you, Alana, not with that man sleeping next to us."

"I don't expect you too, Nettie."

Lynette grimaced, "What if his army comes for him?"

"Then mayhap you should help me so that he may be on his way?"

Lynette's scowl deepened, "I will do no such thing!"

She sighed frustratingly, "Could you at least take Agatha the berries for her husband? I have taught her the elixir, I am sure she can suffice for a time without me."

Lynette was silent a moment before she crossed the room to gather the basket of berries. She paused on her way out to turn back to Alana, "I don't understand your compassion for your enemy, cousin."

The moment she was able, she prepared a fire to exude warmth throughout the hut while a hearty broth simmered within the kettle.

After fetching a basin of water and some cloth, she began to gently cut away the man's bloodied clothing to inspect his injuries.

What awaited her beneath his reddened attire not only startled her but had an unsettling affect on her body.

The sheer size of him relayed his purpose in life. His body was a mass of solid muscle. His limbs stretched well past her makeshift pallet, his arms as well as his legs were immense, his chest a hard wall supporting thick, broad shoulders. His stomach was flat and undoubtedly defined, giving way to thighs as thick as a tree branch. She had never encountered anyone else quite like him.

She remembered earlier when he seized her wrist in a moment of delirium, even than she had felt the strength in his grip, the pain he could inflict with one blow and a thought of doubt flickered in her mind.

Her eyes fell to the punctured wound in his chest and her heart constricted. The blow had been purposefully dealt to end his life; she only prayed that the blade had not severed any vital parts.

After scrubbing away all the blood, she discovered an alarming amount of bruises along his ribcage and imagined that beneath the sinewy muscle the bones were certainly broken.

Most of the damage had been inflicted to the upper half of his body. His midriff revealed a severe mass of cuts and abra-sions, his jaw darkened blue and black from where someone of formidable size had struck him and at the back of his skull was a rather large bump that contributed, along with certain blood loss, to his lack of consciousness.

She was relieved to find that the impact of the dagger had not been as violent as the wound portrayed. Fortunately the Norman's armor had somewhat slowed the dagger's momentum, going in only so far, just enough to sever the skin, leaving torn tissue along the edges but due to the width of the jagged blade, it had stretched the wound considerably into a gaping hole.

She needed to tend the wound quickly before it festered. She cleaned the area thoroughly with warm water and than slowly applied a salve mixed of certain herbs, all the while he remained motionless beneath her tender ministrations, his breathing painfully shallow.

Once she was assured that the wound had been properly cleaned, she knew the worst was at hand. She needed to close the gaping wound and that required using a needle.

She summoned Rowan who, true to his word, had not been far, and asked if he would oblige her by holding the man steady in case of thrashing. Very reluctantly, Rowan agreed and settled at her side as she prepared the needle and suture thread.

Once the tedious task of sewing together the edges of his wound was done, she turned her attention to his sizeable midriff. By the amount of bruises along his ribcage, she was certain the bones were broken, but she had to be sure before binding the area.

Very gently, she reached out and pressed her fingers to his chest, relieved to find that the bronze skin was naturally warm, not feverish and clammy.

"What do you do?" Rowan asked, clearly disturbed to see Alana touch the Norman so formally.

"I am feeling for broken bones." She ignored his heated glare and continued to glide her fingers smoothly over the warrior's flesh and when she discovered his ribs; she pressed firmly and jerked as the Norman released a deep, agonizing groan.

Alana was weary but knew she could not rest until the warrior was restored. She was going to have a long and strenuous night ahead of her.

Chapter 4

He awoke to the awareness of pain. Every part of his body was asunder with throbbing and throe and he found much difficulty in breathing as if a block of stone sat upon his chest, crushing the breath that he found so arduous to produce.

For a moment he lay still, struggling pass the haziness of his mind, staring engagingly up at the turf ceiling, puzzled by the inability to connect his thoughts.

He couldn't seem to focus and make means of anything around him. His body felt heavy, lethargic, his limbs not of his control as he attempted to move.

"You mustn't move." The voice that spoke to him was stern yet soft, and very feminine.

His eyes immediately sought the source of the lovely lilt but he found only shadows cast by a flickering light.

"Who is there?" he growled crossly, groaning inwardly as the room began to tilt uncontrollably. "Damnation-" he clenched his eyes against the excess whirling, "-what did you give me?"

"Tis a sedative brew conjured of ginger root and rosemary. It is for the pain."

His face darkened all the more, "Have you poisoned me?"

There was a soft chuckle, "I assure you, tis perfectly harmless."

As the sedative worked its way through his body, he grew ever more leaden as he struggled to stay alert.

His eyes narrowed suspiciously as he sought the mysterious woman but with the room spinning as it were, it was twice as difficult to fathom his surroundings let alone a woman shifting throughout the room. Unable to fight the strong pull of the brew any longer he blissfully slipped unaware.

When he awoke some time later, he was taken aback by the abrupt splash of sunlight filtering through the room. He blinked several times to adapt to the sudden brightness and felt a lingering effect of listlessness as he attempted to sit upright.

He realized then that beneath the wool blanket, aside from a bandage wrapped securely around his midriff, that he was completely naked.

He gritted his teeth as he shifted his weight, gasping roughly as an intense pain gripped his side in agony. He knew the pain well enough to know that his ribs were broken but how they had come to be in such a state was questionable. He couldn't seem to think pass the obstruction of emptiness in his head. How had he come to be here? Where exactly was here?

He peered around to assimilate his surroundings. The room was fairly large, perhaps a cottage with walls made of wood and the ceiling construed of matted earth. He noticed a wooden chest resting against one wall and an assortment of clay pots aligned along a bench positioned against the opposite wall. A peculiar smell exuded the air and he wrinkled his nose with distaste wondering if the source of the unpleasant odor had been the exact concoction that put him to slumber.

He stiffened at the sound of a man's voice, unfamiliar and distinctly unfriendly. He realized than with increasing agitation that along with his clothing, he had no weapon of use and considering his current state, was not fit to stand against anyone at the moment.

His face hardened with anticipation, his muscles tensing with pain as the door opened producing a youth of average built and dark hair. The boy, not quite a man, lugged a pitcher of water and carried it to place before the hearth; he turned and froze his face hardening with an emotion that bordered intense displeasure.

"So, the Norman has managed to fare."

His eyes narrowed sharply, "So it would seem."

The boy smirked a wry grin, "It would appear that you are in a compromising position, Norman. You are in the hands of your Saxon enemy, what do you plan to do?"

Fallon resisted the urge to sneer. The boy was as arrogant as they came but given the circumstances, he was in no position to inflict much damage, even to a cocksure lad as the one before him.

"Rowan!"

Immediately Fallon recognized the beautiful voice that had spoken to him the previous night but as the boy turned, giving him a visual of the woman, he had not anticipated the sight of what his eyes beheld.

The woman was of slight stature, wearing a blue linen dress with an apron wrapped around an incredibly tiny waist, and small feet adorned in soft leather shoes. Her alabaster skin had an unruly effect on him and he had the oddest impulse to run his fingers to ensure the smoothness of such lovely fairness.

But the most startling feature of this delightful beauty was the peculiar shade of red hair resembling an early sunrise and a kindled flame; a red as lovely as poppies embellishing a meadow.

Alana was intently aware of the warrior's unwavering, golden stare and refused to appear unnerved as she felt within.

Instead, she tried focusing all her attention on Rowan. "What are you doing here?" she demanded her voice surprisingly shrill as she struggled to quell her nerves.

Rowan's face hardened, "I'm here to ensure that this-" at Alana's warning glare he refrained from using terms such as 'beast' or 'savage' and decided alternatively, "-Norman, doesn't harm you."

Alana planted her hands firmly on her waist and lifted her chin to glare pointedly up at Rowan. "I don't need you to coddle me, Rowan."

He stepped closer and she retreated, her face tilting downward at the unexpectedness of his closeness. "Alana-" he began in a hushed voice, "-you tend a man who has come to claim our land."

Her chin lifted once more, "The land belongs to neither him nor you." Her eyes slid sideways to connect with those gold eyes and she quickly looked away. What was wrong with her? She had never been intimidated by a man afore?

Rowan gripped her arm, "I'm warning you Alana, you will bring chaos to this village if you do not send him away."

His words sent a fleeting emotion of fear through her and she wrenched away from him. "Leave me."

He sighed heavily out of frustration but after a hard glance over his shoulder, he quietly left.

Alana turned and felt a foreign sensation tingle through her body. The sunlight poured beautifully into the cottage and it seemed to do wonders for her Norman patient, giving her a clearer picture of the man she had rescued from the forest.

She had never seen such a remarkable man. Incredibly handsome, intensely large, built in an abundance of sheer muscle. Not even Geoff, who was considered the largest man in the village, was nearly as large as this man.

His bronze skin gleamed golden in the light; his tawny-colored hair, swept casually from his forehead, fell in loose waves to rest atop shoulders so wide and immense, she imagined there was not another that could match such broadness.

He managed to pull himself upright, giving her a visual of a lean and intensely muscled abdomen. She felt her face redden as her eyes, of their own accord, slipped even lower to where the edge of the blanket just barely covered his manhood.

"If you continue to peer at me so, as you are, maiden, I may be tempted to act on my own impulses."

Alana gasped and wrenched her eyes upward, stunned to find that the Norman's unyielding gold eyes lingered hotly on her breasts.

Chapter 5

She shivered inwardly for his eyes, in their languid measure of study as they trailed over her, seemed the most startling feature. She had never seen such compelling amber eyes with their uncanny coloration of gold as if all the sun's magnificent luster shown from the iris's of one man.

Alana tilted her chin, determined not to be wavered by such an alluring stare. He had a commanding presence about him, an aura of power that was clearly unmistakable. His golden eyes seemed to unravel her composure and that alone was enough to make her uneasy. She was not one to be easily unraveled.

Her eyes hardened, "It would be wise of you, Sir, to keep your obscenities to yourself."

His eyes danced with a glint of amusement as his perfectly sculpted mouth titled at the corners into a devilish grin. "My apologies milady, I shall attempt to damper my notions."

She eyed him suspiciously, not quite convinced of the sincerity behind his words. Lynette and Rowan's voices clashed in union within her head, warning her that she had made a mistake in bringing this man to their village. Had she truly put her village in danger because of this one man? But what of this one man did she know?

"I would have your word, Sir that you do not intend neither me nor anyone of this village harm?"

His gold eyes intensified with a compressed anger but just as quickly as it appeared it vanished. Had she offended him? "I give you my word."

His compliance came without difficulty and that made her cautious. Though she had argued with Lynette and Rowan about him being Norman, he was nonetheless her enemy and she had to remain vigilant.

She was silent a moment as she weighed his vow thoughtfully. "Do you feel any pain?" she cleared her throat as she crossed the cottage to prepare some broth. She was very much aware of his eyes boring into her back and she couldn't seem to keep her hands from trembling as she reached for a clay pot.

"Why do you do this?"

Alana turned and felt her heart flutter against her breast. His eyes gleamed like burnished warmth, giving her the impression of a fierce lion with his tawny mane and fixed golden stare. "What do you mean?"

"Why do you help me, knowing what I am?"

"What are you other than a man injured at the moment? I am a healer of my people and I have the ability to restore you, and I intend to do so, whether you are enemy or ally."

She paused a moment and added, "You gave me your word that you intend me no harm. I trust in that."

His eyes regarded her with a hint of disbelief. "How can you put so much faith unto me when you know naught of this Norman?"

"Have I a need to be wary of you, Norman?"

He felt a grin tugging at his mouth as he surveyed her amusingly. Despite her delicate size, she had the fiery nature of a man his size and he found himself utterly enthralled by her. "No, fiery one, you need not fear me."

She eyed him for another moment before turning back to her tasks. He found pleasure in watching her, captivated by her lithe movements and agile steps.

She crossed the room and knelt to gather a bundle of bandages. She stood and their eyes met and for a moment she hesitated, her thoughts turning before she finally started towards him.

As she grew closer, Fallon was suddenly struck in awe by the distinguishing shade of green that surveyed him from beneath thick, black lashes. Her eyes were an extraordinary combination of gray tinged with a yellowish green and the more he studied her, the more he seemed mesmerized by her.

Her hands were small and elegant as they slowly worked to unravel the length of bandage but 'twas not her hands that had him intrigued but the perfection of her mouth; full and luscious, a delicate shade of soft pink that seemed to draw him closer despite the unimaginable pain that ripped through him.

He must have groaned aloud for her head jerked upright, her green eyes widening with concern. "Are you alright?" he gritted his teeth at the gentleness of her tone, the velvety softness that wrapped him in sensual warmth as he bit down on another groan.

"I need to change your bandages." She said softly, "Try to not joust about or it will cause you great discomfort."

Fallon resisted a grin, having certain to have never been ordered about by such a small female.

He relaxed his muscles as he anticipated her touch but he had not expected the sudden jolt of desire that flared beneath her fingers, sending tiny pinpricks of electricity along his flesh and inducing a maddening urge to touch her. As absurd as it was, he had to ensure that this lovely creature was real.

He reached out with her unaware and captured a tendril of red hair within his hand. His heart jumped wildly against his chest as he rubbed the soft strand between his forefinger and thumb, amazed by its fiery hue and silk texture.

"Alana!"

Fallon cursed inwardly as he released the lovely strand and his hand fell to his side. He caught her grimace as she turned to glower at the boy fuming at the door.

"What is it, Rowan?"

Fallon caught eyes with Rowan and felt his anger intensify all the more. He was beginning to dislike the lad and with greater reason for the boy was naught but a pompous urchin who thought himself compatible to one of severe prowess such as himself but aside from that, had a possessive gleam to his dark stare as his eyes slid over the woman standing between them.

"May I have a word with you?"

"Can it wait?"

"Nay, it cannot. It is a matter of urgency."

She exhaled sharply but said nothing as she gathered her skirts and got to her feet. Immediately the scent of earth and flowers left him and Fallon cast a heated glare upon Rowan.

He strained to hear the muffled words exchanged between them but could detect naught of their conversation aside from Rowan's angry expression. It was then Rowan gripped Alana's arm as she attempted to turn away, inciting a sudden rage that seemed to flow hotly in his veins.

After Rowan left, Alana returned to his side and proceeded to change his gauze. He watched her in a stretch of silence, very much aware of her hands upon him, creating a flurry of emotions that were not only alarming but exciting for he had never felt such feelings for any woman.

So enraptured by this woman, he had not realized when she finished and started to gather the used bandaging. As she started to stand, his hand lashed out and gripped her arm, and forced a startled yelp from her throat.

Her green eyes widened fearfully as she peered at the large hand wrapped firmly around her wrist. "Have you a need of something, Sir?"

Those words alone seem to unravel him, forcing his thoughts aloud. "I have but one need, maiden, a need that only you could appease."

Her audible gasp resounded sharply in the cottage and for a moment she stood captured within his golden stare before wrenching furiously free of his grasp. "I am needed else where-Norman, so within my time of absence, I think it wise you survey the cottage for your marbles, for it appears you have lost them."

He grinned, "I have offended you."

"And you find this amusing?"

He shook his head as his grin broadened, "What I find amusing is the boy's hopeless attraction for you."

"You know naught of Rowan's feelings." Alana replied angrily, "Nor are they any of your concern." She whirled away from his smirking face, clearly unnerved by his sudden change of nature and the unwarranted feelings he stirred in her.

As she started towards the door, his last remark caused her heart to pulsate madly against her breast; his voice fastening around her like a sensual caress.

"The boy may fancy you but only a man could love you."

Chapter 6

Alana couldn't have been more relieved to escape the confines of her cottage. Something about the Norman with his golden eyes made her heart palpitate in a way that left her breathless and shaky. The rough baritone of his voice, seemed to produce estranged emotions that she had never before encountered.

Willing all thoughts of the golden Norman aside, she focused on the matter at hand as she followed closely at Rowan's heels. Agatha's husband had taken a turn for the worse. The illness had spread rapidly throughout his withered body and Alana feared there was naught more she could do for the village elder.

As she and Rowan approached the hut that Agatha and her ailing husband shared, she was immediately shaken by the putrid smell of death. Her heart quivered apprehensively in her chest as her eyes sought the frail body laying on a corner pallet, an ample woman bent over the incredibly pale man as her sobs resonated through the quiet.

Alana gasped as fear gripped her coldly as feelings of anguish and failure merged painfully to realization.

Hugh was dead. She had failed Agatha. She had failed Hugh. She was a healer was she not? How could she have let this happen?

She felt a strong hand at her elbow, not realizing she had staggered until Rowan steadied her. She shook his hand away and rushed to put as much distance between she and the overwhelming flood of incompetence.

"Alana-" Rowan called from behind.

"Let me be!" she heard herself cry from some isolated part of her mind.

Rowan's hand circled her arm, tugging her to a halt and she rounded on him with anger in her eyes as she shoved roughly at his chest. "Leave me!" she cried loudly.

"Alana, you don't understand-" he started, attempted to dodge her aimless flailing. "-Agatha is relieved."

She froze, suddenly confounded. "Relieved?"

He nodded, "Aye, don't you see? Hugh no longer suffers. You did all you could."

Alana drew in a steady breath, "I could have prevented his suffering."

Rowan shook is head, "Only for a time, my love."

She stiffened at this as the Norman's taunting came back to induce a crimsoned face as his words replayed within her head.

The boy may fancy you but only a man could love you.

She quickly dismissed the taunt and sought an escape. "Where is Nettie?"

Rowan frowned, "I know not, why?"

Alana felt a sudden worry for Nettie was one never to go missing. "When last did you see her?"

Just than, a shrill scream broke piercingly through the village; both Alana and Rowan froze as a woman came fleeing from the trees, her face noticeably pale and her eyes wild with an unmasked fear as she came running toward them.

"Kinsley?" Alana stepped away from Rowan to intercept the frightened girl and gently grasped her trembling shoulders to steady her. "What is amiss?"

"Normans!" the girl cried, "They come, just over the hill!"

A collected amount of gasps sounded as a crowd of curious villagers gathered around them, their eyes growing round with knowing, instilling a look of terror as comprehension settled.

"Are you certain?" Rowan demanded.

Kinsley nodded frantically, her dark curls rebounding against her shoulders as she looked warily around. "Aye, Nettie-"

"Nettie?" Alana's fingers tightened around Kinsley's shoulders with sudden dread. "Where is my cousin?"

"S-she-" Kinsley stammered over her words as panic took root. "-she went looking for y-you, Alana."

Her eyes widened in alarm. If Nettie had gone looking for her that would mean she had taken the same route as the Norman army. "How many Normans are there?"

"Many!" Kinsley cried breathlessly, attempting to wiggle free of Alana's tight grip. "They will kill us all!"

Screams of panic and terror erupted all around her as villagers broken away into a frantic frenzy. Women scooped their tiny children as men gathered weapons while ushering their families into hiding. Kinsley wrenched away and disappeared in the flurry of bodies.

"Come, Alana." Rowan gripped her arm and tugged.

"I have to find Nettie!" she tore away from him and started running.

"Alana!" Rowan's plea was muffled in the outcry but Alana heard naught aside from the violent pulse of her heart beating insanely in her ears.

Curran Macaulay felt a wry grin tug at the corners of his mouth as the cottage door produced a buxom beauty that froze as her blue eyes swept the army planted before her.

He and his men had trailed this route for nearly a day before finally coming upon this small hut and he was certain the remaining village was not far and he had his orders, but what's a little entertainment in the meantime? He would allow his men this one pleasure to ease away the discomforts of the day, he could tell by the hungry glint in their eyes that they needed a little fruition.

His men exchanged looks of intrigue as one by one they dismounted, slowly forming a circle around the Saxon woman. Curran studied the girl; she was pleasing to look at with her honey-colored hair and bright, blue eyes now wide with the utmost fear. She was fairly tall, well-proportioned and had a lovely complexion of ivory.

She whimpered as his men enclosed around her, trapping her and forcing her further away from the cottage.

Otis, a fairly large man with thinning hair, reached out and tugged playfully at a blond strand. The woman yelped and stumbled around falling directly into the arms of Drugo. His man chuckled as his swarthy arms hugged the flailing woman to his chest, her legs kicking in an attempt to escape as he took her to the ground.

She released an ear-splitting scream that caused Curran to wince. "Be easy on the lass, Drugo!" Chimed Olaf as Drugo shoved impatiently at her skirts.

"Cease!" roared a thunderous voice, causing Curran and his men to still.

Curran stared in a state of astonishment at the enraged face of Fallon 'The Fury' as he surfaced from the cottage, bracing his weight against the frame of the door with his face, severely pale and cinched with pain as he surveyed the men in the yard with an intensity that caused several of Curran's men to retreat, leaving only Drugo hovering over the weeping woman.

"'Tis Fallon!" gasped Otis.

"We thought you dead, milord!" said another with incredulity.

Curran dismounted as his eyes moved over Fallon with disbelief. "You're alive." He said this quietly as though in any moment Fallon would vanish into nothing.

"Release the woman." Fallon growled breathlessly, his face twisting with each agonizing breath.

Drugo, very reluctant to release his prize, peered questionably at Curran.

Curran's face hardened. "My men have traveled all day in search of this village; you cannot mean to deny them the spoils of war, brother?"

"I have given my word that no one in this village is to be harmed, and I mean to keep it, Curran. Now release the woman or I shall have your man killed for his insolence."

"Drugo is my man; therefore he is under my command. What is one Saxon wench to sedate his lust?" Curran exchanged a brief nod with Drugo; the warrior smirked knowingly and turned back to the girl, her cries beginning anew as he began to rip eagerly at her clothing.

"My word is law, Curran!" Fallon retorted through clenched teeth as beads of perspiration dotted his forehead and chest; his arms quivering as he struggled to remain standing.

Curran's grin broadened but before he could reply there was a sudden explosion of earth and hooves as a rider and horse broke free of the forest, a pair of small hands wielding a bow and arrow aimed directly at Drugo crouched over the flailing woman.

The horse pranced precariously sideways but the woman in the saddle remained exact, her aim steady as green eyes focused furiously on his man. Curran watched in stunned silence as hair as red as the sun unleashed in the wind before slender fingers lifted and released the arrow.

It whistled through the air with undeviating speed, impaling Drugo clear off his feet onto his back with the end of the arrow protruding from his heart to lay dead at Curran's feet.

The woman on the ground scrambled to her feet as the other ushered her horse forward and extended a hand, all the while, her sage eyes flashing daggers of disclosed rage. She assisted the other onto the saddle and just like that, both women vanished in the obstruction of vegetation.

"Go after them." Curran said smoothly, his eyes fixated on the spot where the red-haired beauty had vanished.

"Nay!" Curran's men froze in their pursuit at Fallon's violent roar. "Let them be." He growled harshly.

Curran's dark brows drew together in puzzlement. "Have you a fondness for your enemy, brother? Have you forgotten your liege who is now King?"

Fallon straightened at this, "Harold is dead?"

"He lies cold with an arrow sticking from his eye."

"Milord-" spoke Otis from the side, "-an army comes."

Curran turned about just to see Fallon's men pouring into the clearing, at this, there was a disgruntled moan of pain and he turned just in time to catch his brother's large unconscious frame.

Chapter 7

Canterbury, England, 1068

There was a great deal of incitement and laughter around him and Fallon sat in the midst of it all and yet was apart from it.

He peered up from the brim of his cup, the ale barely consumed as he surveyed his clan as they conversed with serving wenches and sipped merrily from their beakers. An assortment of food lay dispersed along the trestle table but Fallon found little appetite to dispatch of any of it.

His troubled thoughts carried him away, to a place where he'd rather be, a place where it 'twas only him and a red-haired beauty.

Alana.

He had dreamt of her many nights, his mind continuously tormented with the memory of earth and flowers, of a silken strand of red hair that had glided so smoothly between his fingers, of lips so delicate a pink, he ached to taste.

Every pain in his body brought on her memory; the image of a Saxon maiden whose compassionate heart had revived him, and yet had stolen a piece of him.

There had been countless women since that time, but none could appease the insatiable desire for the fiery beauty that had stolen his heart.

His fingers curled tightly around his cup as he was brought back to the day he awoke to find him in a bed that was not a makeshift pallet and to see a woman of plain countenance tending his wounds.

Soon after he had been informed that the Saxon village had been burned to the ground and naught remained but soot and blackened debris. Most of the inhabitants of the village had escaped and only a few men were killed in defending what was now a pile of ashes.

When he first learned of this, he was overcome with a maddening rage. He had given a promise and that promise was broken. A village was destroyed and several villagers lay dead and his mysterious Alana, had vanished.

"What troubles you, milord?"

Fallon blinked to awareness and peered to the man at his left. Ranulf had been his right-hand man for some years but foremost his trusted companion. He was a bear of a man with a barrel-chest that bore more scars than one could count. His hair, naturally dark was kept shaved thin to the scalp. His roughened face bore a large nose which from previous brawls, was hooked and a prominent scar that cut clear through his right brow. His voice was thunderous and tremendous, instilling fear in those who did not know him.

They had reason to fear him. Ranulf was a short fuse; his manner aggressive and at times intractable when driven to madness. Any reason to brawl was a good enough reason. Many viewed him as an intense man with scars, a battle-hardened man that thrived in combat and pain. Fallon knew the man well enough to know that his scars went deeper than the surface and that combat was a means of release.

Aside from his beastly appearance and aggressive nature, he was unquestionably loyal and impeccable in battle.

"Ah, he thinks of his pretty lass." Goaded Ivan from his right, his eyes glinting like sapphires with a hint of humor as he lounged casually in a chair, his legs crossed comfortably atop the surface of the table.

Ivan was as impulsive as he was reckless with fine aristocratic features that fooled limitless women into believing he was as charming as he appeared. He was a beguiling youth that came and went as he pleased, never committing and entertaining his days with inquiries. He was tall and exceptionally lean with a cropped due of mahogany hair and a square chin and straight nose. His easygoing manner tugged on the patience of others but his skill in battle compensated for his impulsiveness.

Smirking a wide indifferent grin, Ivan reached over and slapped Fallon coolly on the back as he motioned to the women in the room. "Have you a pick, Chieftain?"

Fallon grumbled irritably as he lifted his beaker and drank of ale. He eyed the women in the room from over the brim of his cup but neither was of interest to him.

Ivan chuckled lightly and shrugged his lean shoulders as he kicked his feet down to the floor and strolled from the hall.

"If you'd like, I'll skewer the bastard and be done with it."

Fallon's mouth stretched into a grin as he peered at the man now settling into Ivan's chair. He was not nearly as large in stature as the others but what he lacked in size he made up for in prowess and wit.

Gavin was the soundless sort, usually occupied with his thoughts but occasionally he would spat a few retorts.

Fallon took immediate notice to the pairs of female eyes drawn to the man at his right. Gavin was just as aware of the attention he received as his hazel eyes moved appreciatively over the women eyeing him.

"Have you word of William, my liege?" Ranulf asked, changing the matter.

Fallon inhaled a deep breath as he set his cup down and a dull pain surfaced in his chest. Even after several months of revitalizing there was still a moderate ache that would resurface time and again.

Since the battle at Senlac Hill, William had devoted all his attention to his accomplished land. He had engrossed himself in building structures of stone all throughout England, the first being built at Hastings, wasting little time in establishing order.

For their aid in battle and the downfall of Harold Godwinson, William granted all his knights land and title, disposing Saxon landowners of their keeps and instilling them with Norman knights.

Fallon was granted ownership of Linden keep. It was a magnificent fortress with high stone walls and large round towers and an extended curtain wall that trailed the outside walls.

When he first came upon the sadly composed structure when given mastery over it, it's previous inhabitants fleeing the structure at word of his arrival; it was barely a structure of weak walls and rotted timber. With as much time and devotion, he and his men quickly set out to rebuild what was now a formidable fortress, erect to withstand any imposing force. It needed much more constructing and various inanimate objects to fill its empty rooms but in another year's time, Linden would be complete.

A servant entered the hall and bypassed the serving wenches. Fallon peered up from his untouched plate as the man appeared at his side. "Milord, a missive has arrived for you." He extended the enclosed letter.

Fallon accepted it and dismissed him. He ripped open the seal and scanned the scrawl with narrowed eyes.

"What is it, my liege?" Ranulf asked curiously.

Gavin leaned forward, noticing a sudden tension around Fallon's mouth.

"My presence has been requested by a Lord Emerson McLeod."

Gavin frowned, "McLeod?"

"He is Saxon." Growled Ranulf distastefully.

"What does he inquire?" Gavin asked.

"He wishes to enlist me in a matter concerning his land."

"His land?" Ranulf scoffed.

Fallon smirked, "He says his allegiance is with William."

"Hah!" Ivan expressed loudly as he sauntered into the hall. "No Saxon is loyal to the Conqueror."

Fallon held up his hand and the room fell silent, "I have reason to believe this man is true to his word. He claims the matter is important. Ready the horses."

Chapter 8

Castle of McLeod

Lord Emerson McLeod paced the enclosure of his grand hall, his brooding thoughts bringing about a continuous treading along the stone dais beneath his feet.

He was a statuesque man of reasonable size, sporting a thick mane of black hair and eyes equally dark that corresponded with a long, shaggy beard; his harsh appearance alone had struck fear in many but in just a year's time the number of adversaries had grown to an alarming rate despite his fearsome disposition that generally was reason alone to keep enemies at bay.

He was renowned for his abundant currency and tenacity merged of iron that had provided him ample prestige and a monumental band of mercenaries that had been entirely loyal to him, but in a fleeting turn of political events his impressive artillery had dwindled precariously due to countless attacks by Norman invaders, leaving his stone walls weakened.

In fear of losing his lands and keep to a Norman, he had personally sought the one called Conqueror and in a desperate attempt to keep his lands, he declared his allegiance; vowing to serve his new King to the utmost degree so as long as he was to remain Lord of McLeod keep.

With much relentless persuading, the Norman King reluctantly agreed to grant him his appeal, but with his request came a severe price, a price that would surely see him asunder, but he had little choice in the matter, 'twas this or he would lose all that which belonged to him.

The bargain arranged between he and the Conqueror himself had prompted his irregular pacing. He was not a man accustomed to fear and even now the foreign feeling sat heavily in his belly, churning over and again as he replayed their words of agreement in notion.

He heard a sudden scuffle outside the doors of the hall and froze to a standstill as they swung wide and his messenger came forth, his elongated face taut with apprehension. "Milord-"

"Macaulay has arrived?" his throat was thick with foreboding as the words seem to weigh on his tongue.

His servant nodded, "Shall I show him in, milord?"

He nodded and regained his pacing. He had dreaded this very moment the day the agreement was arranged. There was no turning back; he would do anything necessary to ensure his status, even if that meant coming face-to-face with the acclaimed Fallon "The Fury".

Since the Conqueror's rise, he had heard much speculation on the notorious Norman warrior that had fought diligently by William's side.

Emerson felt an unsettling tremor pass through his body. "The Fury" was known for dismantling men with one cleave of his blade. He had heard the dreaded name in the winds that whisked over the hills; the name of a man believed to be indestructible and otherworldly.

It was said that the Norman had encountered death itself and prevailed. He was called by many names but "The Fury" was most fitting for it 'twas rumored that his temperament, when provoked, cued a blind haze of red and all rationality fled for naught but destruction lay in wake.

Emerson inhaled a deep breath, straightening his spine in an attempt to appear undaunted as the doors of the hall opened wide; revealing a man of colossal stature and eyes an unnatural gold and a countenance of suppressed rage.

He forced a slight grin to his face as he stepped down from the dais and motioned to a chair, "Laird Macaulay, please make use of anything that appeals to you."

The Norman's face darkened grimly as he said, "There is naught of this place that remotely appeals to me, McLeod. I have but one interest of matter and 'tis that reason alone that I have come. You claim it was of grave importance so do me the courtesy of cutting the minimal details and explain for my presence here."

McLeod tampered down a sudden flare of irritation at the Norman's brazenness. He had to keep in mind that this was not just an unspecified Norman but the Fallon "The Fury", the blade of William the Conqueror.

"I have pledged loyalty to your King."

Those golden eyes narrowed doubtingly. "The Conqueror does not show lenience unto his enemy."

"I am your enemy no longer." McLeod assured.

"You claimed this was a matter concerning your land and it would appear that my King has not stripped you of them which would mean an agreement was arranged."

McLeod nodded and folded his arms behind his back to still the trembling. "We McLeod's are an esteemed and feared unity; my keep has not been breached for nearly a century. I have an army of formidable size. I am an asset to this country."

"Your self-praise is wasted on me." Macaulay growled. "What does this have to do with me?"

McLeod continued, "My lands have been unapproachable for some time but since the Conqueror's reign, I have had countless attacks and I fear I am unable to withstand much more. I pledged my allegiance to your King in exchange for the right to keep my lands and title."

A golden brow arched, "You were born a Saxon and yet, you abandon your heritage so carelessly? That is not honor."

McLeod's eyes hardened, "I do what is necessary."

He snorted in ridicule, "You may have pledged your loyalty to my King, but time will reveal the truth of your words."

"That is why you are here." McLeod retorted, "You are here to test the truth of my words."   Fallon stiffened, feeling a sudden uneasiness but he said nothing as he waited.

"Your King has much faith in you, Fallon "The Fury", so much faith that he would seal you to a Saxon."

Fallon felt a sudden feeling of entrapment. "What nonsense do you speak?"

McLeod turned and began a leisure pace, "To ensure my loyalty, the King has ordered an arranged marriage." He paused and met those feral, gold eyes. "You, Fallon "The Fury" are ordered by your King to marry my daughter, the Lady Rosalind, to guarantee my sincerity."

He felt his anger rising as his hands curled tightly into balls of fists. "My King has not informed me of any of this."

"It was your King that ordered it about. I am much against it as you are, Macaulay but as much as it sickens me to admit; I am desperate and need a means to keep my clan intact."

Three fierce strides brought "The Fury" to loom above him and his face reddened with unmasked fury. "If you speak with a false tongue-" he said in a disquieting tone, "-I will return with haste to sever it without qualm."

McLeod felt his face pale considerably beneath the gold-inflamed glare. "I speak the truth." And than added quickly, "Give me but one moment."

He slipped cautiously by the enraged warrior, feeling as if his very body scorched to the touch with the violence streaming through him. How would he ever cope with sealing his daughter to such a man?

Fallon felt every muscle in his body teeming with disbelief mixed with rage. How could William bind him to a Saxon without his consent?

He had no desire to marry. Even as he thought this, Alana's face flickered to mind. He growled inwardly for the mere thought was infuriating. He could not seem to rid himself of her memory.

He was not a man construed for matrimony! He was built specifically for war; had been trained for that alone since he was a lad.

Yet, in the back of his head, the thought of a woman to call his own, bearing him children gave him reason to pause and again her face came to mind.

So absorbed in his thoughts, he had not heard the doors opening until McLeod called him to present. "Macaulay, I wish to present your betrothed, Lady Rosalind."

He turned around to survey the woman revealed to him. The girl, not nearly a woman, seem to shrink with fear beneath his angry stare. She was fairly tall and slender with curves of little interest to him. Her hair, swept into a tight chignon at the nape of her neck was as black as a raven's wing. Her sloe eyes seem to study him with a mixture of appreciation and fear.

She held her hand to him, expecting him to take it. He stared down at her hand, unmoved. He thought of another woman with hands so small, so gentle in their tending and quickly banished it.

Without a word, he swept past his betrothed with her hand still hovering in the air and a panicking McLeod as he stormed from the hall, the door slamming with deafening force.

Chapter 9

Fallon received word that William had reached Lincoln and there had issued an order to destroy nearly over a hundred Saxon homes to begin constructing a new stronghold of timber, rumored to have two mottes.

So enraged by this arranged marriage, he thought of naught else but to seek his liege and demand reason.

When he arrived to Lincoln and came upon the sight of the magnificent fortress constructed from the hands of previous Saxon titleholders he found himself at awe with William's eagerness to conform England.

At word of his arrival, he and his men were greeted by a squire who immediately took their horses and they were led from the outer bailey to the grand hall.

"Fallon." His name was spoken on as a raspy welcome as Fallon and his men dropped their heads to honor their King.

William stepped forward, dressed in a tunic beneath links of chain that crossed his thick chest and brown woolen breeches that narrowed at the top of his leather boots.

Beneath a set of thick, dark brows shown eyes of intensity that Fallon had grown accustomed to since he had served William at fourteen.

William was a man who showed little to no emotion; reflecting a steel disposition, instilling fear in those who dare rebel against him.

"How goes the assembling of Linden keep?"

"As expected, my liege." Fallon straightened to add, "May I have a word of private, milord?"

William nodded and dismissed the servants. Fallon exchanged looks with his men and one by one they quietly left the hall, leaving the two of them.

"Something troubles you?" William asked as he motioned to a chair.

Fallon settled down across from him. "You arranged a marriage without my consent?"

William's expression remained impassive. "I did."

Fallon felt his temper rising. "Why?" he grounded between clenched teeth.

"You have served me well, Fallon Macaulay, and 'tis time that you settled and take a woman to wife."

"I have no need of a wife." He growled, "Especially a McLeod."

"McLeod is one of the most feared and influential men of England and he has sworn fealty to me."

"He is Saxon. There is many that rebels against you, what's to say he will not do the same?"

William arched a thick brow, "You must have some semblance of trust in the man for you answered his missive, did you not?"

Fallon remained silent. He did not trust McLeod, but a part of him, in the back of his mind, thought of the burned Saxon village, the one he had sworn to protect and failed to do so. Somehow, he imagined this would appease the guilt.

It did not.

William took his silence for an answer. "I ordered this marriage because the woman has a considerable dowry that will please you. I have ordered him to give up his daughter to a Norman warrior of my choosing to seal our bargain. If he so much as violates our agreement, he will be stripped of his lands and cast out like all the rest.

"I do not have the time or patience for a meek wife."

William smirked, "You will one day wish for a bairn to succeed you, no?"

He had not given children much thought.

William rose to his feet, as did Fallon, his face furrowing with indignation as he struggled to keep his anger at bay. "It does not please me to make you unhappy, Fallon. You have served me at best and nearly lost your life fighting for England. I shall give you time to familiarize yourself with your betrothed."

"And if she does not please me?"

William turned, his face darkening. "I am merely giving you a chance to become acquainted, so that when you do marry, you shan't be strangers."

Fallon bit down on an angry retort.

"Do we have an agreement?"

"Aye, my liege." This was said darkly.

William's eyes hardened as he added, "I am a man of my word, Fallon. If this treaty is violated, I will see fit to punish those who cross me."

Once more, he said nothing but merely nodded.

"Aside from that, there is another matter I wish to discuss."

"Milord?"

"Your brother seems to have a fondness for raiding."

Fallon groaned internally. "I am unaware of Curran's affairs, my liege."

"I would think it wise you restrain your brother's disorderly ways. I have had word that he continues to attack the villages, stealing valuable goods and raping the women. He does this on a whim and it does not please me to have more enemies."

Fallon nodded, "I will see to it, milord."

"See that you do, because if his madness continues, I will put him to ground, whether he is kin or not."

Fallon left Lincoln more discouraged than when he arrived. His men were silent the remaining journey back to Canterbury, taking note of his blackened mood.

His first thought when arriving back to Linden keep was to find his impish brother and bring a stop to his plundering; his newly McLeod bride being the furthest from his mind.

"You sent for me, brother?" this was said more with ridicule than curiosity as Curran sauntered into the hall, his gray eyes assessing the room icily.

Fallon stood and surveyed his younger brother with growing vexation to his indifferent approach.

Curran was exactly the obverse, down to his dark features that were in startling contrast to his golden visage, the only feature in slight comparison was the same prominent nose.

He had always known his brother to be cold and detached from the world. He thrived in bringing destruction unto his enemy and inflicting pain on those he thought deserving of it so it came as no surprise to him when William declared he had been raiding.

He motioned to a seat, "Sit, Curran."

Curran's face darkened with contempt, "I don't take orders from you, brother."

He dropped his hand, "So you are a man above decree?" he growled.

Curran smirked as he moved to the table and poured himself a beaker of ale. "I am man of many things."

"Why did you attack those villages? They are defenseless against your army and had no cause for destruction."

Curran's gray eyes glinted like steel as he replied, "Have I need of a cause to take from my enemy?"

"William is not pleased."

"It was done simply to show that William is not to be trifled with."

"You did it simply out of amusement. If you continue your attacks William will view it as treason."

"And have me beheaded, I presume?" Curran mocked.

Fallon's eyes narrowed to slits of burning embers. "You will attack only if William issued the order, understood? In the mean time, you will do well to cease your jesting and abide."

"Then what do you suggest, brother?" he said this lightly.

Fallon exhaled sharply. "You and your men will reside at Linden keep-"

"Ah-" he grinned, "-to ensure I am an obedient dog."

"Curran-" Fallon growled impatiently, "-I do this because you are my brother."

"Half-brother." He replied callously.

Fallon stiffened with anger, "I am giving you a direct order, Curran. You and your men are under my command; I am chieftain of this clan and there is no one that would say otherwise, whether you wish to acknowledge that or not, you have little choice in the matter but to comply."

He felt the fury pouring from Curran in waves but he said nothing, merely nodding before stalking from the room.

Fallon breathed a sigh of exasperation as he turned and swept a hand through his tousled hair.

His brother was indeed a challenge in itself.

He could only hope that his bride-to-be was not as challenging.

Chapter 10

Despite a great deal of unwillingness to marry the McLeod wench, he undertook the finishing touches on Linden keep, making some semblance of a homely atmosphere aside from its formidable outward facet.

Linden keep was home to the Macaulay clan and as of now, it was naught but a cold, empty structure.

He gave the task of filling the empty rooms to his chaplain, Egan, who handled his expenses and commodities. It wasn't long before a range of woodwork and assortment of items began to embellish the floors and walls.

Rich tapestries adorned the windows and wall brackets held candles to light the corridors. Trestle tables dotted the grand hall with linen coverings and wooded benches on either side. Each room brimmed with fine-crafted furnishings of massive beds made with overlaid mattresses with thick coverlets and feather-stuffed pillows; bureaus and chests occupied corners and lush carpets covered the cold stone floor.

Before too long, there was naught else that needed improvement within the walls while on the outside, much construction continued and as extravagant as his keep became with all its lavished objects, it lacked domestics.

Late one evening, while dining in his hall, a letter arrived. The letter was a written plea from Lord McLeod, his betrothed's father.

Fallon grumbled beneath his breath as he scanned the scribble with growing agitation.

There had been another untimely attack on the McLeod fortress, this invasion nearly succeeding in breaking their walls. He claimed the attack was led by Ralf 'The Red' Lechmere.

His nostrils flared with increasing annoyance. Ralf 'The Red' was no threat to him but a grave hindrance to a Saxon, especially those unwilling to give up their land and he was well assured McLeod's resistance prompted Lechmere's attack.

In his letter, McLeod pleaded for his aid in this matter, claiming his betrothed's life was at stake.

Fallon slammed the letter onto the table and cursed William beneath his breath. He felt as though he were already chained to the McLeod wench. She was his betrothed and any threat upon her was a threat upon him, whether he liked it or not, he would have to bring an end to these attacks.

Gathering to his feet, leaving the letter to rest upon the table, he went in search of his knights and asked his newly squire to prepare the horses.

Lechmere Keep

Ralf 'The Red' Lechmere hoisted his hefty frame from his wooden chair and strolled across the room to survey the fine crafted sword presented to him.

His thin lips curled approvingly beneath a bulbous nose as he reached out and gingerly traced a stubby finger along the sharpened blade.

"Ah-" he purred, "-splendid."

The small craftsman standing below him gave a pert nod and slowly entangled the sword from Lechmere's fingers. "The blade is double edged and slightly tapered. It is six centimeters wide and forty inches in diameter. The hilt is devised of gold." The little man spoke proudly, his beady eyes moving admiringly over his art work.

Before Lechmere could praise the small man for his fine craftsmanship, a serf appeared to announce unexpected visitors.

Thick, russet brows grooved to the center of his wide forehead as he stepped back from the craftsman. "Who has come?" he demanded sharply.

"He says his name is Macaulay." The serf responded tentatively.

Lechmere stiffened his face paling at the name. He cleared his throat and dismissed the craftsman, the sword no longer of interest. "Show him in."

Macaulay. What reason did 'The Fury' have for seeking him?

He heard the advance of footfalls and turned as his serf entered followed by four large, menacing men, a face in particular revealing a hardened resolve.

"Laird Macaulay, you must forgive the disorderliness of the hall, I was not expecting visitors. Do what do I owe this honor?" he peered at the three brooding men standing behind Macaulay. "Please, sit and have a drink." He flicked his fingers to a thin man standing aside. "Get these men a drink." Lechmere ordered.

Fallon exchanged a glance with his knights and nodded. Gavin and Ivan were eager to settle into a chair but Ranulf hesitated before doing so. Fallon remained standing.

Lechmere was a burly man with a mane of matted red hair and eyes a distinct coffee brown. "You have come to speak of trade?"

Fallon shook his head. "I am here to speak on the behalf of Lord McLeod."

Lechmere's russet brows drew together with puzzlement, "Saxon McLeod?"

Fallon nodded, "Aye."

"I would think you of all people would not associate with the enemy, Macaulay."

He felt his anger rising as he inhaled a deep breath through his nostrils. "McLeod is no longer an enemy of our country. He has claimed fealty to our King."

"I did not have word of this." Lechmere said, "You are certain of this?"

Fallon nodded, "I was informed that McLeod's land had been attacked, these attacks were supposedly led by you, is that fact?"

Lechmere nodded, "He refuses to give up his land."

"The attacks are no longer necessary. McLeod is to remain untouched."

Lechmere's eyes narrowed with suspicion, "Why do you defend this Saxon?"

"His daughter is my betrothed." He replied with vexation.

Lechmere blanched, "'The Fury' is to marry a Saxon?"

"With much reluctance, I assure you." He grumbled. "It was arranged by William himself to ensure McLeod's loyalty." Why did he feel it necessary to explain this to Lechmere?

Lechmere chuckled lightly, ""The Fury" is to take a wife? I pity your betrothed."

Fallon felt a grin tugging at his lips. "Indeed."

"You have my word, Macaulay, McLeod shall remain un-scathed." he settled into a chair and relaxed as he swept a hand toward the opposing chair. "Please, sit, you and your knights may have a meal before you depart, no?"

Fallon peered at Gavin and Ivan who characteristically had helped themselves to a pitcher of ale with a Ranulf observing them beneath hooded eyes of displeasure.

He nodded and settled next to Ranulf and in the next hour as the meal was in preparation, they discussed William and their attained country.

"Ah-" Lechmere expressed with glee as the servants flowed into the room, bracing silver trays loaded with an assortment of food.

Fallon's stomach grumbled noisily as servants crowded the table and began setting trays before them; in this abrupt-ness, a tray was suddenly toppled over, clashing loudly with the stone floor and spilling its remnants all over Lechmere's lap.

Lechmere bellowed a sudden vicious wail as he shot to his feet as the scorching food burned his thighs.

As an initial reaction, Fallon was afoot and followed Lechmere's angry leer to a woman standing between them. He stilled for something about the woman, whose back was to him, seemed vaguely familiar.

She felt his golden gaze upon her and slowly turned. His eyes grew round with realization for the blond woman was the very woman Curran's men attacked that day at the cottage, the very woman Alana had rescued from their clutches.

Chapter 11

Lynette stiffened as horror washed over her and she took an involuntary step backward. The warrior with his golden eyes was larger than she remembered and far more menacing. He stood motionless and just watched her with a look of awareness.

"You bitch!" thundered Lechmere and she spun around, startled by his anger as he attempted to brush the herring pie from his lap.

Fear clutched at her chest as Lechmere raised his hand. She stepped back, forgetting the Norman at her back, and braced herself for the pain.

When his hand did not fall, she opened her eyes to see Lechmere's hand fastened in the Norman's iron grip.

"Do not raise your hand to her." She felt the rumbling of his voice vibrate through his massive chest and realized in her fear she had backed into him.

She immediately straightened her spine to keep from touching the warrior and turned back to Lechmere. "M-my apologies, milord." She tucked her head downward and peered at his booted feet, caked too with herring pie.

Lechmere's eyes glinted angrily above her head at Macaulay whose grip remained firm. "You can release me, Macaulay."

Slowly, the fingers unfurled and his hand fell away.

"I should whip the clumsiness out of you, wench."

Fallon felt the woman stiffen before him but she said nothing, not even a faint whimper to express her fear.

"Where is the other?" he demanded and the woman spun about, her blue eyes wide with alarm.

Lechmere frowned, "Other? What other?"

"The red-haired woman." He said this without taking his eyes off the girl.

It took Lechmere a moment but than he said, "Ah, you must mean the defiant one!" This caught his attention and he averted his eyes to Lechmere. "She's a spirited one, the wench."

"Where is she?" he demanded forcefully, catching Lechmere unaware. "Where is the woman?"

Lechmere's dark eyes sparkled with sudden curiosity, "You have an interest in the Saxon wench?"

"Is she here?" he growled.

Lechmere was silent as he weighed this considerably, suddenly puzzled as to how Macaulay had known of the red-haired woman. "Come with me." He said and started from the room.

Fallon exchanged a meaningful look with Ranulf and the big warrior nodded as a silent trade of words passed between them.

His heart beat an unwavering rhythm of anticipation as Lechmere led him through a narrow corridor and turned to ascend a winding stairway of stone.

Alana.

Her name brushed the walls of his mind like a sweet caress. How could one woman, a Saxon at that, have such an alluring pull on him?

Many nights he tossed restlessly in his bed, thinking of hair the color of sunlight and eyes an unusual shade of green but most of all, the kindness she had bestowed him. Would he find that kindness still?

They came to a stop before a wooden door with an iron latch. Lechmere stood in front of him and fumbled to unlock it. It took every ounce of patience in his body to not shove the man aside and see to the task himself.

Finally, the lock released and the door slid ajar.

The room was absolutely stifling. The four walls that imprisoned her seemed to grow smaller every day. She had paced the stone floor for what seemed a sennight but was uncertain of the actual amount of days that had passed.

She would have suffered a thousand lashings to this! She felt like screaming and crying all at once; much more of this and she would surely go mad!

Lechmere had grown exceedingly impatient with her defiant nature and shoved her with a smug look on his face into this dreadful, stuffy room.

As she paced the floor, her brown skirts billowed widely about her ankles as she thought of a scheme to escape Lechmere. Her last failed attempt had brought her to her current imprisonment and she vowed not to fail again. Somehow, she would get Nettie and herself away from this place.

She had come across crueler men than Lechmere, but he was a Norman nonetheless who made his distaste for Saxons quite evident.

She exhaled sharply through her nose as she spun around; her thoughts turning with ways on how to flee Lechmere keep when she heard a noise from the corridor.

She stopped suddenly and sought for an object in the room. When she spotted the steel mug that had contained her drinking water from earlier, she rushed forward and grabbed it from the floor.

She crossed the small room and pressed her back against the wall and waited, listening intently as Lechmere's voice carried from the other side. The latch rattled beneath his ministrations and the door swung inward.

Her heart pounding roughly against her chest, Alana had not given thought to the other man who trailed behind Lechmere but instead jumped forward and brought the steel mug straight down onto Lechmere's head.

As Lechmere staggered away from her, she turned to flee only to collide roughly against a wall of chain mail.

A startled yelp escaped her throat as strong, calloused hands caught her upper arms, bringing her to an instant halt.

Her mouth fell open into a distinct O as her green eyes surveyed the man looming above her and she gasped, "You!"

Fallon felt a grin tugging at the corners of his mouth but resisted as Lechmere stumbled sideways and he caught a flash of red as the object of his thoughts came running directly into his arms.

Instantly the scent of earth and flowers wafted to his senses, stirring his blood in a most affective way. His fingers tightened ever so slightly around her, preventing any movement which she seemed incapable of doing for she merely stared at him with astonishment blazing angrily in her sage eyes.

She was more beautiful than he remembered. She had twisted her red hair into a plait which dropped delicately over one shoulder, tiny stubborn strands escaping their restraint framed her flushed face and he found himself completely drawn to her lips, wanting in that moment to taste them.

"You damned wench!" cursed Lechmere as he pressed a hand to the knot forming atop his head.

Alana, still stunned to see her golden Norman, turned slightly as Lechmere started towards her. She tensed but just as he raised a fist, the strong hand on her arm pulled her back and the Norman's huge frame stepped between them.

"I would speak with you in private." Fallon interjected.

Lechmere grumbled disapprovingly as he glared at Fallon and than Alana. Grimacing with pain, he dropped his arm and proceeded out into the hall.

Once in the corridor, Fallon demanded, "How much for the Saxon woman?"

Lechmere, slightly taken aback peered at Fallon as if he had gone daft. "You wish to purchase the fiery wench?"

"And the flaxen-haired."

Lechmere hesitated, "I would gladly sell you the fiery one but the flaxen-haired stays. She is not so troublesome and I could use a wench to warm my bed."

Fallon shook his head, "I'll not leave without the other woman. I'll pay you considerably for both and toss in a few furs. My offer stands."

Lechmere fell silent. If he denied the offer than he could possibly offend the warrior, and to make an enemy out of 'The Fury' did not sit well with him.

"I suppose I can find me another wench." And than thought, what better way to punish the fiery wench than to hand her over to the devil himself?

Chapter 12

Alana was in disbelief. She had tried many times afore to put the golden warrior from her mind but since that day she had stumbled upon him in the forest; his image seemed cemented in her mind.

He had played her for a fool, indeed, having led her to trust in his word and what good did that do? Her village was now ashes in the wind! What an utter fool she had been! He had deceived her, the despicable blackguard!

They had warned her that he was a barbarian and she had disregarded caution and the error of that had nearly destroyed Nettie.

The vision of Nettie straddled beneath the Norman warrior as he ripped aimlessly at her clothing burned vividly in her mind. She would never forgive herself for trusting the enemy so carelessly. She vowed never again to let her heart interfere.

As she paced before the closed door, wondering at what the two men could possibly be discussing, she felt her temper flare. She wanted to pummel the Norman's chest until her anger was spent! She wanted to scream out all the heartache of her village now soots! Innocent villagers were dead because of his men!

She had detected Lechmere's hesitation around the Norman and wondered mindfully, did Lechmere fear the golden warrior? She realized than she knew naught of the man, including his name but what did that matter?

The door opened and she turned to face the Norman as he stepped into the room, his golden eyes burning with an emotion she could not fathom. Lechmere followed closely behind and as he stepped around the warrior, his mouth widened into a satisfying sneer. "Gather your belongings, wench, for you belong to 'The Fury' now."

'The Fury'!

Had she heard right?

Her eyes slanted towards the golden man in her peripheral. Surely this man was not the 'Fury'. She had heard unimaginable tales of a man whose adeptness in battle bespoke of a man incapable of conquering. Many Saxons died from 'The Fury's' blade; slain without qualm and as her eyes moved fleetingly over that golden face, she trembled within. How could a man, whom she had tended and once detected tenderness within be the man known for sheer ruthlessness and a fiery temper likened to the blazing sun?

"You stone deaf, wench?" Lechmere growled, "You best move with haste lest I change my mind and keep that bonny kin of yours for myself!"

Alana stiffened and averted her green eyes from the gold-en warrior to Lechmere. Her eyes hardened as she blurted, "You will not touch her!"

Lechmere, taken aback by her sudden brazenness, re-sponded instinctively and brought his hand across her cheek with enough force to knock her off her feet.

Alana reacted naturally, fueled by the explosion of pain, scrambled to her feet and rushed at Lechmere but in a swift and fluid motion, a large brawny arm stopped her flight and Lechmere felt the tiny prick of a double-edged blade pressing beneath his jugular.

"I gave you fair warning in mishandling the women-" Alana felt a tremor race down her spine for the gruffness in his voice relayed his ire and for a moment, she believed this man capable of the tales spoken.

Lechmere's throat convulsed nervously beneath the pres-sure of the steady blade as he glared pointedly at Fallon and said through grounded teeth. "I shall leave you to get better acquainted with your newly obtained slave." he said this lastly with a leveled look at Alana before gingerly stepping away from Fallon and leaving the room.

Still enraged at Lechmere, Alana did not realize that the Norman still held her firmly against him, his muscular fore-arm pressing intimately beneath her breasts.

An immediate flush stained her cheeks as she wiggled out of his embrace. She whirled around to face him and glared heatedly into those gold eyes which surprisingly were alight with warmth. She frowned for if this man was truly the 'Fury', she knew the warrior to be incapable of compassion.

His golden tresses trailed the length of his chiseled face, and she seemed drawn to his perfectly sculpted mouth. He appeared far taller and much larger than she remembered and beneath his pressing gold eyes, her eyes swept hastily down the length of his stalwart frame.

"You must learn to subdue that curiosity, maiden, for in your once-over, I find myself plagued with compelling impulses that I find troubling to ignore."

Alana stiffened, remembering that day in the village when he had spoken nearly the exact remark, and she was surprised by the velvety smoothness of his voice when only but a moment ago, his tone had been baritone and laced with fury. "So I am to be your property now?" she demanded, her green eyes narrowing sharply on his rugged face.

"You do not seem pleased." She detected a slight playfulness in the undertone of his voice.

"Should I be?" she questioned, eyeing him distrustfully.

A golden brow arched curiously as he asked, "Would you prefer the likes of Lechmere to mine?"

Her chin jutted upward, "You Normans are all alike."

She noticed a slight tension forming around his mouth and sudden change in his demeanor. "You make a moot point, fiery lass, one that will be further scrutinized in our time together."

Her solidified expression signified her anger. "Whatever your means for me, you will find that I do not comply without difficulty, Norman." This was lastly said with sheer indignation and Fallon struggled to conceal his mirth for despite her certain hatred for him, he found her irresistible in all her heated contempt.

Damnation, she was beautiful. He found his defenses faltering for those sea-green eyes seem to burn right through him. He had expected to find the gentle maiden who had tended him so gently but in her place was this passionate woman teeming with a fire as red as her hair and he certainly agreed with it.

Unable to resist, he stepped towards her and her face furrowed with sudden anxiousness. "It would please me to have you in my bed."

His curt remark prompted a sudden outrage in Alana, "Than you shall be sorely disappointed for I have no intention of sharing your bed!" she snapped.

Her back came upright against the wall and she gasped, realizing he had cornered her for now the only obstruction standing in her way to the door was the sizable mass of muscle standing firm before her.

She was forced to peer up at him and tilting her head back she glared directly into those gold eyes burning with unveiled desire.

He reached up and grasped her chin gently between his forefinger and thumb. She attempted to jerk away but his grip tightened, instilling a sudden unease in her. Her heart thumped wildly in her chest for his honeyed gaze rested hungrily on her mouth.

His tawny head tilted downward and Alana froze realizing the big brute intended to kiss her! She seemed riveted and unable to resist for though her mind demanded she turn away, her body seemed immobile to do so.

The moment his lips captured hers, she felt a warm fluttering sensation in her belly and something foreign tug at her heart. The gentleness in his kiss startled her for she had expected viciousness, but his kiss only deepened with eagerness and his tongue swept delicately inside, encouraged by her inexperienced response.

Suddenly, images of her burned village rushed to mind and the spell was broken. She shoved desperately at his chest and pressed herself against the wall to escape the tantalizing pressure of his lips.

He was the enemy, she had to remind herself. She couldn't allow him to deter her from her anger. He was not to be trusted.

His hands ensnared her wrists and beneath the amount of chain mail, she felt his heart beating avidly in his chest and as she peered into that fervor gaze, she detected a struggle within.

A scream erupted from somewhere within the keep, shattering the quiet and Fallon felt Alana stiffen immediately as fear clouded her green eyes.

He did not think twice on releasing her for the scream had come from the flaxen woman and the moment he did, Alana swept past him and rushed from the room.

He drew his sword from its scabbard and followed into the hall.

The sight that met him forced an unexpected grin to his lips for Ranulf, a man of extreme size, had never looked so perplexed and uneasy as his friend struggled to control the flailing flaxen lass and attempted to ward off Alana's sudden attacks as she wrestled with the burly warrior to free the other.

Off to the side, Ivan catered to the ale in his hands with a wry grin stretching his face as Gavin watched the scene with a bemused expression on the flaxen-haired woman.

Noticing Lechmere observing in the corner, the man merely surveyed the display with growing agitation.

Perplexed and ready to depart Lechmere keep, Fallon rushed forward and snatched Alana around the waist, pulling her abruptly off Ranulf.

"What goes on here?" he demanded, his arm latched tightly around her waist as she struggled to break free.

Ranulf, still slightly dismayed by the sudden chaos, peered at Fallon with chagrin. "My apologies, my liege-" he started, his voice gruff as he paused to maintain a grip on the woman twisting against him. "-this chit has gone mad!" he exclaimed angrily.

"Let her go, you brute!" Alana demanded, her green eyes bestowing a vengeful glare on the massive, scarred warrior.

Fallon was astonished for most women cowered before Ranulf because of his beastly appearance but she appeared undaunted.

Fallon averted his gold eyes to Ranulf and said, "Release her."

With much eagerness, Ranulf released the woman and stepped away. She dropped to the floor, spent and breathless, and Fallon reluctantly did the same and Alana rushed to the woman's side, gently running her hands up and down the woman's spine for reassurance.

As his eyes rested on the two women, he asked, "What happened here?"

Ivan was the first to speak. "The woman tried to leave the room."

"I merely stopped her." Ranulf added surly.

Feeling a need to defend the woman, Gavin quickly cut in. "She was frightened."

Alana suddenly shot to her feet, her green eyes blazing as she glared hotly around the room. "Of course she's frightened! She was left alone in a room with Normans!" she spat harshly.

"Enough!" Fallon growled, "Gather the horses. We leave for Linden."

Chapter 13

Alana glanced over her shoulder at Lechmere keep disappearing over the hills. She was relieved to leave Lechmere but her relief was short lived for what was she to expect now that 'The Fury' was her new lord?

She shivered inwardly as she surveyed 'The Fury' beneath lowered lashes. The sun making its slow descent cast golden strays of sunlight upon his tawny head, enhancing those wavy tresses to a lustrous hue.

What about this Norman had her heart pounding erratically? At the remembrance of their kiss she felt a deep crimson stain her cheeks and quickly drew her eyes away.

But it was his kiss that had stirred a curiosity to explore the passions he awakened in her.

Don't be so naïve, Alana. She warned herself, remembering painfully the consequences of trusting her heart. He was the reason her village now lay in destruction.

She cast one last glance at the golden Norman and was startled to see him watching her.

Her heart fluttered chaotically against her breast as she quickly looked away and focused on the setting sun.

"Do you think he is as cruel as they say?" Nettie asked from behind.

Alana had been utterly surprised when they were given a horse to share and knew he had done it in their best interest considering Nettie's fear of Normans, but was quick to notice that the Norman did not trust them so easily. All four Normans surrounded them the moment they mounted the mare. An escape on horseback at the moment proved futile but escape had crossed her mind.

"I know naught." She whispered, remembering Nettie's question. "Just stay quiet and I'll think of something."

She turned her head and was startled to see one of the Norman's staring at Nettie. If not for the circumstances, Alana would have considered the warrior remarkably handsome. He was not quite as large as the other three but physically lean with kempt hair the color of wheat with a perfectly aligned nose and a distinct angular chin.

His hazel eyes seem drawn to her cousin and she detected warmth in them but she was wary of his attentions for nevertheless, he was Norman.

They traveled well into the night and Alana found herself drifting asleep in the saddle. A shadow fell in at their side and Alana jolted awake, her eyes connecting sleepily with gold eyes.

"How much farther?" she asked wearily.

"There is a glen up ahead, we will rest there for the night and continue in the morning." His gold eyes moved past her shoulder and settled on Nettie.

"Your friend sleeps. Mayhap you should let Gavin relieve you of her weight."

Alana straightened in the saddle to glare more firmly at him. "I am fine."

Those gold eyes narrowed with admiration. "You are very fond of her. She is your sister?" a tawny brow arched.

"She is my cousin." Her green eyes peered over his shoulder to Gavin, "And it would be wise of you to inform your men to not touch her."

"My men will not touch her unless I issue the order to do so."

Alana grew apprehensive as she studied him with sudden wariness. "And do you intend to ravish us, milord?" she was taken aback by the softness of her voice, her fear heightening all the more when he did not hasten to reply.

"Milord, shall we make camp?" Ranulf intervened as their horses entered the small valley.

His gold eyes rested intensely on Alana as he replied, "Aye."

As they settled into camp, Alana watched the scarred warrior produce a small fire. The warrior who had taken an interest in watching Nettie busied himself with the horses, tying their reins to tree branches while the third warrior sauntered into the shadows, whistling under his breath.

Alana's eyes found the golden Norman and for a moment, she wondered at his name. He stood at a magnificent height, every ounce of his masculine frame equipped in rippling muscle. She found herself inexplicitly drawn to watching him move about.

He had discarded his chain mail and wore a white linen shirt that outlined every distinct muscle that made up his forearms. The sheer breadth of his shoulders and chest were twice the size of others and his trousers molded to thick thighs, giving way to his leather boots. She had never witnessed a man of such proportion. If he were equipped for anything in life, battle seemed most fitting.

When he turned, she realized his direction and quickly looked elsewhere. Her heart began thumping irregularly in her chest at his approach and she struggled to appear impassive to his presence.

"Have you a need to relieve yourself?" his frankness caused Alana to grimace and catching this, Fallon resisted the urge to grin. "Have I offended you, milady?"

Her expression hardened as she gathered to her feet. "Your presence alone offends me, Sir."

As the two women started towards the entrance of the forest Alana was stunned to find that the Norman followed closely behind.

She whirled around. "What do you think you are doing?" she demanded.

He smirked, "You do not honestly think I would let you go alone?"

"Of course!" she snapped. "Do you honestly think we would try and flee in the dark?"

"The thought had crossed my mind." He peered at the other woman who merely watched the two of them with alarm.

"You will have but this one moment to relieve yourselves, so I suggest you tend to your needs for the chance will not arise again until we reach Linden keep."

Fuming silently, Alana turned back around and ushered Nettie forward. She was grateful that the Norman had enough sense to turn away but in that moment with his back turned to her, she swept a fleeting glance around her, wondering at an escape. If she attempted it would certainly be risky. Would the two of them be able to accomplish such a feat without getting caught?

She brushed thoughts of escape from her mind for she was unfamiliar with the territory and didn't know of the dangers that awaited two vulnerable women. At least with the Normans, she and Nettie had some security but once the opportune moment arose, she would not think twice on escaping.

They made their way back to camp and found a spot by the fire. Nettie quickly settled down and fell into a deep slumber. Alana, slightly on edge, sat protectively at her cousin's side and peered around the camp.

The scarred warrior studied her from across the fire and she quickly averted her eyes, unnerved by his dark stare. The other warrior whose hazel eyes had studied Nettie earlier, slept soundly to her far right.

She felt the relentless pull of exhaustion and unable to ignore it any longer, settled down beside Nettie and allowed a moment to rest. As her eyes fluttered closed, she was instinctively aware of his presence nearby and for some unexplained reason was comforted by that.

Alana awoke some time well into the night. As her eyes partially opened, she could see the fire burning low, the tips of the flames barely breaking the surface of the timber. She blinked away the sleepiness and was suddenly aware of a chill at her back.

Rolling over, she was startled to find Nettie gone. Gasping aloud, she scrambled to her feet, her eyes moving frantically around the circle of sleeping men. With her heart hammering against her chest, the only sound perceptible to her ears, she turned to survey the darkened foliage.

Surely Nettie hadn't chanced the forest? But Alana knew her cousin well enough to know that when overcome with fear; she was unpredictable which prompted irrational decisions.

Exchanging a wary glance between the wood and sleeping Normans she wondered if she should risk it? But the thought of Nettie out there alone, facing the unimaginable dangers that awaited a helpless woman, caused her heart to lurch.

Sparing one last glance over her shoulder and seeing that none of the men had stirred, she started into the blackened forest.

As she started her ascent, she called out softly, hoping her cousin would be nearby to hear but when silence answered, she continued, her steps slow and unsure of the earth beneath her.

Panic began to take place for what if something dreadful had happened to Nettie?

The forest suddenly came alive with clamor. A gasp wedged tightly in her throat as she spun about, abrupt noises sounding in all angles, twigs snapping, animals scurrying and she found herself stumbling through the thickets with fright.

Nettie! She wanted to scream but feared she would give herself away. Had the Normans arisen to find them gone? If she were caught would 'The Fury' punish her?

There was a sudden thunderous crashing of vegetation and the distinct murmur of male voices. Her panic rose to hysteria and fearing she would get caught Alana turned and began to run.

She slapped blindly at extended branches as their finger-like tips struck at her face. She could hear the ends of her skirt snagging and ripping as she swept past protruding limbs and her hair untangled from its restraint fell in loose waves down her back.

She heard an abrupt splintering from behind and momentarily startled by the noise, peered over her shoulder and collided roughly with a solid shadow.

The moment her hands contacted warm flesh, she cried out as the earth rushed up to meet them. In the sudden momentum, her attacker turned to brace the fall and she landed softly atop him.

He grunted at the impact and realizing she was perfectly unharmed, Alana lifted her head and her eyes connected with a pair of burning, amber eyes.

Startled, she scrambled to get to her feet but as quick like a stealth cat, 'The Fury' shifted left, rolling her beneath him.

She was suddenly very aware of the male contours pressing intimately against her; every sinewy muscle of his chiseled frame now lay flush atop her, with his hand cradling her head. She knew he held some of his weight to keep from crushing her and with his arms trapping her; she had little choice but to peer directly into those gold embers.

She had expected his fury but instead got silence. The quiet as well as the uncanny gleam in his amber eyes unnerved her.

"Why did you run?" he asked softly, his gold eyes searching her face.

She detected tenderness in him and it confounded her. "You startled me." She replied and then realizing he made no inclination of moving she asked, "Are you going to let me up?"

He was quiet and that prompted her heart into an erratic pace. His gold eyes settled on her mouth, parted in her labored breathing, she caught a flicker of desire before his tawny head leaned forward and he lightly pressed his mouth to hers.

The touch of his lips sent her heart spiraling madly out of control. She lay motionless beneath him, reeling in the elicited emotions cued beneath the caress of his pursed lips. He kissed her with a startling gentleness, catering to the corners of her lips and abandoning her mouth to trail hot kisses down the length of her throat.

It was when she felt a cool draft on her bare skin that she realized he had hiked up her skirt and his fingers splayed the length of her thigh. Her heart slammed against her chest and she stiffened beneath him.

"Nay!" she gasped, pressing a balled fist to his chest.

For a moment, he seemed in a trance, his gold eyes glazed with a fiery haze and slowly the fire in his eyes dimmed, but she knew his desire still burned beneath the surface.

She had to gain some semblance of control on her emotions and forcing the unbridled urges down, her green eyes hardened with disdain, "Let me up."

His face hardened to an implacable resolve and she regarded the man whom many feared but he remained quiet as he gathered to his height. He grabbed her wrist and jerking her forcefully to her feet; she stumbled and landed in his arms.

Catching her breath, Alana pushed poorly at his chest but his arms remained firm. He leaned close and the masculine scent of spices and wood assailed her senses, inducing that warmth that seemed to spread through her limbs like hot liquid.

"When we make love-" he said hoarsely, drawing a labored breath from her throat, "-you will not fight me but come willingly to my bed."

The chuckle that surfaced from her throat was not as convincing as it sounded as she struggled to remain aloof to his assertion. "That day, Norman, will never come to be."

Chapter 14

Alana made sure to keep a lengthy distance between her and the Norman cur trailing behind her. Her lips were still swollen from his kisses and her thigh seemed to burn from where his hand had touched her. She was finding it extremely difficult to remind herself that he was her enemy.

As they neared camp Nettie's screams shattered her resolve and she split into a run, heedless of the man behind her.

When she burst into the clearing, she took in the man, who earlier had watched Nettie with an unusual leer, struggling to maintain a fruitless grip on her cousin.

She noticed the remaining two Normans, the scarred warrior and the other with an amused expression, merely watched in vain, neither willing to assist their companion.

When the Norman made no move to release Nettie, Alana started forward but a large, callused hand grabbed her arm, stopping her. She started to jerk from his grip but his fingers tightened.

"Let her go, Gavin." He commanded, and just like that, the blond-haired warrior released Nettie and stepped away.

When Alana attempted to step toward her cousin, the hand on her arm stayed her and she cast a dark, meaningful look up at him but his amber eyes rested on Nettie with indifference as he said, "Whatever the reason behind your fears, girl, you may be well rest-assured that my men and I have no intention of harming you or your cousin but if you attempt to run again, I shan't be lenient."

Fallon was stunned to see an intensity of anger flare in the flaxen-haired eyes when all along he had thought her meek and a trembling sort. "Do we have an understanding?"

"Mayhap you should order your men to keep their hands to themselves?" Alana snapped, drawing his attention. "She doesn't like to be manhandled."

His temper rising, he turned to fully face the spirited beauty that sparked a fire within him. Even now with her staring angrily up at him with those sea-green eyes and tendrils of flamed-hair framing her face, seem to kindle his desire.

"She's going to be manhandled if she struggles. My men have not harmed her, but if she insists on running then that leaves us little choice but to drag her forcefully back to camp-" pausing he peered mindfully at Alana's cousin and than Gavin, "-I have it in mind that for the remainder of this journey, your cousin is now Gavin's liability."

Alana opened her mouth to protest but the Norman was quick to cut her off. "I will hear no objections. You two have caused enough trouble for the night and I wish to make it to Linden in peace."

"Please, Sir-" Alana was startled when Nettie spoke up for her cousin had barely uttered a word since leaving Lechmere keep. "-I will not attempt to run again. I am merely frightened-"

"And you would leave your cousin to fend alone if we are such barbarians?" Fallon growled.

"I do not fault her for running." Alana was quick to say and she truly didn't but the sudden look of guilt on her cousin's face was clear-cut.

Alana noticed the fire seem to reflect in those golden-amber eyes and for a moment he appeared unworldly.

"Ranulf-" Fallon shifted his attention to the giant, scarred warrior. "-you will take next watch. Gavin, you and the woman will take position by that boulder to rest and if necessary, tie her ankle to yours." He said this lastly with a hint of warning.

As the scarred warrior disappeared in the forest, the other Norman who had taken first watch settled comfortably before the fire and Gavin, Fallon had called, lightly placed his hand at Nettie's elbow and motioned her toward a spot before the boulder.

The large male frame at her side shifted and Alana peered into those gold eyes as he said in a hoarse tone for her ears alone. "You are going to keep me warm for the night."

His hand ensnared her elbow and pulled her along. The thought of sleeping next to him all night made her heart jump erratically against her chest and remembering quite vividly his kiss in the forest, she wondered if he would try at another attempt with his men sleeping on the other side of the fire.

He settled down into a soft patch of grass and stretched out his long, muscled frame. He peered up at her with a slight wry grin and she had a sudden impulse to kick him square in the thigh, but she would probably do more damage to her foot than his muscled thigh and decided against it.

Inhaling a deep breath, her gaze wavered to her cousin who had settled next to Gavin, who surprisingly, had not tied her ankle to his.

"He will not hurt her." Alana peered down at the golden Norman, a look of sincerity etched severely in his face as he watched her. "I give you my word."

She stiffened for what good was his word? He had once given his word that no harm would come to her village or villagers and that had proved to be a lie.

"Alana-" he was growing impatient for she could clearly see lines of fatigue forming around his eyes.

She settled down beside him and rolled onto her side away from him. His arm fell across her and she gasped when he dragged her back against him. Startled by this, she wrestled to put space between them but his gruff voice stilled her struggles.

"Be still, I only mean to keep you warm."

She went still but it was a long time before she was able to fall asleep.

He may have lied to the fiery lass, claiming he merely intended to keep her warm for what he truly longed to do was lay her beneath him and have his way with her.

He reveled in the moment, having her small, soft body cradled against him. He knew she did not sleep, for her body was as rigid as stone, but he had no intention of 'manhandling' her, as she had called it earlier and dammit if he wouldn't suffer!

The length of her hair fell softly across his arm and a gentle breeze teased the red tresses, causing the strands to move caressingly against his skin.

That intoxicating scent of earth and flowers permeated his senses and a maddening rush of yearning for the woman in his arms nearly drove him wild with wanting. It took every ounce of his self control to not explore her enticing frame and so he groaned inwardly for this was going to be one long, hellish night.

When he awoke the next morning, the sky was a mere stretch of gray; the sun hadn't yet to crest the mountains.

Immediately he was aware of the warm, feminine body nestled at his side. He bit down on a sudden groan, his breeches uncomfortably tight as he shifted his weight onto his elbow to peer earnestly at his Saxon beauty.

She had turned in her sleep and was curled against him. Her hair, that vibrant shade of sun-kissed roses, framed her sleeping face in dispersed, silken strands.

Irresistibly drawn to that unusual shade of red, he reached out and captured a wayward strand, stroking the intricate tress between his fingers.

For a moment, he merely watched her sleep, captivated. She was Saxon and yet, he did not view her as his enemy, but rather, as the compassionate woman who had taken a chance in saving a Norman, whose spirit burned brighter than any man or woman he had ever encountered.

Her distrust of him confounded as well as displeased him. Her sage eyes burned with an anger that was as deeply puzzling and though he admired the fire in her spirit, he wondered as to the gentle beauty that had tended him so gently. What had brought about this detachment in her?

Releasing the silken strand, he arose to his feet before the others roused and quickly sought a task to engage his thoughts.

An hour later, as they carried on with their journey to Linden, he found much difficulty in keeping his eyes from straying to Alana. He vowed than and there, at any cost, that he would conquer the fiery lass, even if he were at risk of losing his own heart, one day she would belong to him and him alone.

Alana could feel the Norman's bold, amber stare and as unsettling as his golden eyes were, they seemed to incite a spark of excitement and curiosity. Her instincts warned her to stay clear of 'The Fury', but a stray inclination implied that he was not the monster many believed him to be.

If he was such a barbarian, why had she not witnessed such characteristics when she saw to his wounds? Yet, there must be a reason behind his sobriquet?

Remembering her village in ruins and the lives destroyed, her heart hardened to any soft emotions towards the Norman. What did she know about him, aside from the terrifying tales spoken, and those brief days in the cottage, she knew nothing.

She wondered then, what reason did the Norman have for purchasing her and Nettie from Lechmere, and suddenly, her cheeks reddening with the remembrance of his retort the previous night had recalled the foreshadowing of his words.

When we make love, you will not fight me, but come willingly to my bed.

The promise in those heated words brought a blush to her cheeks. She would not succumb to his advances, whatever his reason for her, whether it be serf or bed wench, she would not submit without a fight but in the back of her mind, there was a flicker of doubt concerning her feelings.

The sight that greeted her as they trailed over the rolling hills caused her heart to shudder in awe. The commanding stronghold constructed of stone made a reeling indention against the bright, blue sky but as they continued, it was the small village nestled below that grabbed her attention.

There was a sudden clamor and the growing number of peasants swarming the open road gave Fallon and his men reason to pause.

It was the sudden crack of a whip that brought Alana upright in her saddle, gripping the pommel with unease followed by a woman's abrupt cries.

As the ominous sound of a whip struck through the air, making its mark, Alana watched Fallon dismount, his mouth twisted into a grim line.

Without a thought to whether he would object, Alana swung down from her horse and followed him into the thick crowd.

As he shoved his way through, the peasants, realizing who he was, grew alarmed and swept from his path with alarming haste.

The horrid display that met there path caused Alana's face to pale considerably beneath the midday sun.

Five swarthy warriors stood in a wide circle, their eyes glinting sharply on the peasant strung up in the center. The man's shirt lay tattered at his feet; blood seem to streak his marred back in rivulets, the skin completely torn and shredded from the impending lash.

Alana pressed a hand to her mouth, her eyes widening as they traveled over the man who, barely conscious, struggled to keep his legs from buckling beneath him. His body trembled from the damage the lash had already inflicted and the remaining punishment he was to receive.

Alana noticed that one of the warriors held a squirming young woman against him, her struggles futile as aimless tears streaked her face, her large, round eyes riveted on the man in the center.

"What goes on here?" Fallon snapped and immediately the crowd seem to part from him.

Alana stepped up from behind him and noticed that one warrior in particular, holding the hilt of the ominous whip, had his back to them.

The dark-haired warrior slowly turned and it was all Alana could do to not flinch beneath the cold, silver eyes settling first on Fallon, and then with surprise on Alana.

Chapter 15

"What goes here, Curran?" Fallon demanded his face a mask of barely suppressed rage.

Alana's eyes hardened as the man called Curran stepped toward them, his silver-gray eyes taking on a wolfish gleam as they trailed leisurely down the length of her.

She felt her stomach twist beneath his bold perusal and lifted her chin to glare more directly at him. Her defiance seemed to only excite him further for his mouth curled cruelly at the corners.

An inclination warned her that this man was very different from Fallon; the aura around him seemed dark and merciless. Something in her heart told her to be wary of the warrior.

She knew she had other reasons to fear him. Sparing a glance over her shoulder, she was quick to notice that Nettie had gone deathly white in the saddle. These were the men that had attacked her cousin. His men, she thought, her eyes settling on the golden Norman at her side.

"Answer me." Fallon growled.

"I am merely doing what you have failed to do." Curran snapped, drawing his attention away from the woman. "Do you condone your peasants to live freely on your land?"

Fallon's face darkened noticeably, "What do you say?"

"He is a pathetic farmhand. He has not paid his dues and his fields are lacking." Curran smirked inwardly as he added, "He has little regard to your decree."

"Nay, milord!" cried the helpless woman struggling anew against her captor. Her dark eyes pleaded mercifully with Fallon. "Please, milord, my husband has taken ill and has been unable to work-"

Fallon held up his hand to silence the woman and immediately her face went ashen. Alana's heart quivered against her chest. Surely he wouldn't punish the poor farmer because he was ill?

Fallon turned to Curran, "You should have waited for my return." He said without emotion. "What's done is done. The man has taken his punishment."

Curran's expression darkened with censure. "Your leniency is wasted-" he said low enough for only Fallon and Alana's ears alone. "-you need to make an example of them." He fell silent and waited for Fallon to do so, but when he did not, this only seemed to anger Curran more.

Turning sharply, he handed the whip to one of his men standing off to the side and approached the farmer's young wife.

Alana's heart wrenched against her chest as he grabbed the woman by her hair and jerked her against him.

"Curran!" Fallon growled dangerously, his big body teeming with fury.

The woman cried out as she struggled against him but Curran seemed unaware as he turned dark, stormy eyes on Fallon. "If you refuse to make an example, then I'll gladly oblige you." With that, he reached down and unsheathed a small dagger and brought the blade to the girl's throat.

Alana reacted on pure instinct. Her heart demanded she intervene and it took little convincing. Reaching down, she grabbed the large hilt of Fallon's sword and drew it from its scabbard. She had not anticipated how heavy the sword would be and nearly faltered beneath its weight, but the girl's soft pleas empowered her and she moved with a deftness that surprised even her.

Pressing the sword into the man's back, she spoke with an even calmness that was just as startling as her agility in wielding the blade. "If you so much as draw a drop of her blood, I will not think twice on severing your spine."

A stunned silence settled over the village and even Fallon had not moved. He stared in complete awe at the fiery Saxon who showed little to no fear in challenging a Norman. If there were any signs of fear; it was for the girl at Curran's blade.

Fallon was well accustomed to the sword's weight and though he wielded it with ease, he knew a woman of her size would be unable to support it for long. Her arm began to tremble with its heaviness but her severe expression remained intact.

Delighted at the turn of events, Curran slowly brought the blade away from the woman's throat and very carefully turned to access the flamed beauty glaring intensely up at him with sharp green eyes.

No woman had ever challenged him and the excitement it aroused brought on a flourishing stimulation for the small woman before him. She was indeed a challenge, a challenge he had every intention of conquering.

His silver eyes glinting with a challenge, he said to Fallon without taking his eyes from her, "Where did you find her, Fallon?"

Fallon. She was quick to note the golden Norman's name.

Something in the way Curran spoke and how his eyes traveled over Alana's body brought on a sharp pang of jealousy and rage. He knew his brother well enough to know that once his eyes took on that uncanny gleam, he was determined to get what he wanted and from the look in his eyes, he wanted Alana.

"Enough!" he growled more forcefully than intended. "Curran, you are out of line. Take yourself from my sight lest I take the whip to your back myself!" he turned his gold, livid stare onto Curran's men. "If you do not heed my warning, I will do unto you what has been done here. Understood?"

Curran's men grudgingly nodded and hastened to their horses. Sensing their Lord's unrestrained fury, the villagers moved forward to untie the beaten man and assist the whimpering woman who had scurried away from Curran.

His anger barely controlled, Fallon moved forward and grabbed the sword from Alana's wavering hand and turned his heated stare on his brother, "If you were not my brother, I would have you punished for taking the law into your own hands, from now on when there is an issue concerning my tenants, you will come to me. You sought to make an example and in doing so, shamed me."

Curran's gray eyes hardened icily. "I meant no disrespect, brother." The words spoken, Alana detected, were without sincerity. His silver eyes wavered back to Alana and she stiffened, "I shall leave you to your business." And with that, he stalked away.

Alana froze for those gold, amber eyes, abundant with fury, were now directed at her. She had never seen him so angry and realized her mistake in not heeding the tales spoken of 'The Fury'.

She was suddenly wary of the punishment that awaited her.

He said nothing and that heightened her fears but she would not regret what she had done. She could not withstand an innocent woman suffering all because of debt! She would take whatever punishment he intended and with that thought, lifted her chin determinedly.

Fallon was aghast with astonishment but he kept the emotion well concealed beneath his hard resolve. She had openly defied him and challenged a Norman all for the sake of a peasant's life and the fiery look in her eyes dared him to scold her, if not for his maddening fury, he almost would have grinned.

Taking her arm a little too forcefully in his hand, he jerked her along. When she started towards her horse, his grip tightened and he pulled her in the direction of his horse. "I think not, lass. You are to ride with me until we reach the castle. You will not stray from my sight for I intend to have a word with you."

Alana's heart jumped against her chest and she was beginning to grow uneasy. The warning in his words was clear but she vowed not to sway beneath them.

Taking her tiny waist in between his hands, he lifted her effortlessly into his saddle and mounted up behind her. Grabbing the reins, and attempting to ignore her tempting bottom cradled between his thighs, he steered his horse towards the castle.

As they entered the bailey, all thoughts of the happening in the village vanished as Alana focused on the commotion around her. She caught sight of a chapel and inhabitants flowing too and from the building. There was a storehouse which she knew contained dry goods and barrels of wine and ale. She heard the clamor of steel on steel and turned her head to see a burly blacksmith hammering away in his workshop. She detected, within the air, a diversity of smells from baked bread, to furnished hay and horse manure.

Numerous buildings occupied the three acres within the curtain wall and Alana was stunned to see such a homely place. She had thought only Kings lived as such. As their horses came to a stop and a small boy rushed forward to take them, Fallon reached up and lifted her from the saddle, and once her feet touched the ground she noticed his hand remained firm around her arm.

He turned to address Ranulf with Gavin trailing behind, gingerly holding Nettie's arm. "Ranulf, you will see to the woman."

The scarred warrior nodded and turned to take Nettie from Gavin. Alana instinctively knew her cousin's reaction to the battle-hardened warrior would be one of fear and she moved to intercept him but Fallon restrained her.

She rounded on him with anger, "Your man will frighten her."

He simply ignored her and Alana turned to somewhat comfort her cousin. "Go with him, Nettie. I'll join you shortly."

Fallon didn't give Nettie a chance to respond but instead jerked Alana along after him. His grip tight on her arm, it was all she could do to not stumble after him. She was growing angrier by the minute in his treatment of her and vowed to pummel him if she had the chance.

She barely had time to access her surroundings with him dragging her along as they traveled a poorly lit corridor, passing countless rooms; he finally came to a stop before one and tossed the door wide.

Her heart thumping loudly against her chest, he pulled her into the room and released her, slamming the door with deafening force.

Somewhat startled by this, she turned fully around to face him, rubbing her arm where his fingers had been a moment ago.

His gold eyes settled hard on her as his massive chest rose and fell with his anger. "Do you realize the danger you put yourself in?" he growled hotly.

She was taken aback by this, she had expected his anger but not for this reason. She jerked her chin upward and met his leveled stare. "I find no fault in aiding those helpless."

"You had no right to intervene." He snapped.

Her green eyes darkened with anger, "You made no move to assist the woman. I refuse to see an innocent murdered all because of debt. It is barbaric!"

"It is not your place, Alana."

"I will do it time and again if the opportunity were to arise." She snapped, suddenly enraged. "You are a heartless cad if you intend to stand idly by and allow such cruelty to occur!"

She realized her mistake in taunting him for he enclosed the space with such unanticipated speed that it brought a yelp from her throat. He gripped her arms in between his large hands and held her firm beneath his intense, amber eyes.

"Any other Lord would have whipped you senseless for your daring." His voice was soft yet throaty, as though the words pained him.

Alana couldn't have been more aware of his male presence and she suddenly felt a twinge of fear. Standing immobile in his large hands, she forced the words from her throat. "If you intend to whip me, Norman, then I pray you be done with it."

She was unnerved by his silence and the way his gold eyes studied her with an intensity that seem to burn right through her. "You want me to whip you?" he asked, almost incredulous.

She raised her chin and responded simply, "Aye."

Fallon studied her carefully. He had never wanted a woman as badly as he wanted Alana. She challenged him at all costs, even now, with her sage eyes openly defying him; her red hair framing her small face in a silken wave beckoned his touch. She showed little fear to her wellbeing when it came to others and damn him for wanting to punish her for her impulsiveness, but she had to learn there were repercussions for acting foolhardily.

She wanted to be whipped but that was the furthest punishment from his mind. His gold eyes settled hotly on her lips and in her green eyes he detected a flicker of fear.

"I see fit to punish you in but one means." The husky lilt in his voice was all the warning she received, his hand fell to her waist and jerked her roughly against him.

Her hands immediately fell to the wide expanse of his chest in an effort to push him away as his other hand entangled itself in the length of her hair. She opened her mouth to protest but her cries were muffled by the sudden invasion of his lips. He intended to be rough, to teach her a lesson in being foolish but the moment his lips captured hers, his kiss softened, and his tongue pushed past her lips to sweep delectably within.

As his kissed deepened, a gruff groan erupted from his throat as he pushed her further back into the opposing wall, pressing her solidly against him, and he relished in the softness flushed against his hardened body.

He released her hair and his hand spanned her waist, marveling at how small her midriff appeared beneath his large hand. His fingers trailed along her narrow ribcage to settle eagerly beneath the swell of her breast. She whimpered against his mouth and his lips trailed hotly along the delicate line of her jaw. He felt the strength in her waning and this only encouraged his hunger.

His other hand slipped around her waist to cup her enticing bottom, forcing a startled gasp from her throat. She maintained her struggles but with his body and the wall trapping her, she could do no more than shift against him, arousing him further.

She felt her senses fleeing chaotically as his mouth trailed hungrily over her skin, planting hot kisses against the hollowness of her throat as his hand cradled her bottom, flattening her hips against the swollen bulge in his breeches.

Alarmed by this, she pushed against him, struggling to control the unwarranted feelings he stirred in her.

Every burning impulse in his body demanded he continue, his throbbing manhood ached for release, but he paused, remembering the reason beneath his longing. He had never wanted a woman as badly as he wanted her and it took every ounce of control he had to release her.

The moment he did, she stumbled out of his reach, her beautiful face flushed with anger, her lips swollen and bruised from his kisses. For a moment, he thought he detected a glimmer of yearning that reflected his own, but it was quickly dismissed with a sudden storm of fury. Had he imagined it?

"Norman cur!" she spat, her green eyes blazing. "I've told you to never touch me!"

Struggling to maintain his control, his hands curled into fists at his sides as he said with a warning and a hint of eagerness, "If you do not learn to control your hasty behavior, milady, you shall receive more than what was given today."

She stiffened, "So I am to be 'The Fury's' doxy?"

He felt an impish grin tugging at the corner's of his mouth. "That all depends on how you intend to behave." He replied huskily.

Her eyes narrowed to slits of green ice. "I shall defy you at every turn, Norman."

He grinned suddenly, "Then expect to be in my bed."

Chapter 16

For a time, Alana could do no more then glare angrily at the door, the last of the Norman's words replaying in her mind and the searing remembrance of his kiss left her just as swayed as his promised retort.

Fallon.

The golden Norman was a mystery. How could one warrior have such a startling affect on those surrounding him?

His golden appearance and proud disposition conveyed an image of a powerful, tawny lion. His eyes of that unusual amber glow radiated such power and command but beneath that hardened, golden exterior, she sensed a man worth knowing.

A sudden tremor raced down her spine at the image of the opposing man from the village. The man called Curran reflected the very opposite of his golden brother. She struggled to believe that, that man could be kin to 'The Fury'. His eyes had held no warmth, no detection of compassion for human life. His eyes, as silver and ghostlike as the moon and hair as black as the night, reflected a sly, black wolf.

Alana nearly laughed aloud of her comparison of the two men but the more she pondered the thought, she knew there was no denying that the men were as untamed as their reflected predators and with that followed a sudden, wary notion.

Which man should she fear more-the wolf or the lion?

Fallon stalked the corridors, seeking to put as much distance between he and his Saxon hellcat. She was a fire under his skin and as much as he longed to ignore the searing effect she had on him, there was no denying his immediate attraction to Alana. No woman had ever troubled his thoughts or had such a magnetic pull on his desire but something about the fiery lass stirred him in a way that others had failed to do. He was no wet-behind-the-ears kind of lad and was accustomed to having women in his bed, but Alana was an unlikely sort, the kind he had never encountered. It was obvious from her heated words and angry-sage eyes that she harbored some sort of animosity for him. He intended to unravel her reasons for her anger and discover the woman who had tended him so gently in the forest.

He was not the sort of man familiar with pursuing women but if any woman was worth chasing, Alana would be his match.

The thought of having her in his bed was such an intriguing thought he nearly groaned aloud. He imagined her fiery tresses splayed across his pillow and her body arching to his caresses as he claimed her.

He had not given much thought on what he would do with her once they reached Linden. He had thought of no other woman since that time in the village and now that he had her in his possession, he could think of none other than having her in his bed but he knew it would not occur without fight. His fiery Saxon had no intention of becoming his thrall, let alone his bed wench.

She would attempt to escape, of that, he was certain and there were many outside the Linden walls that would take pleasure in seizing a fiery prize as his.

The thought of another man touching Alana heated his blood. He would skewer a man without hesitation if they so much as considered it. The thought was as confounding as it were maddening but he knew without doubt he would sever the earth to ensure her safety.

He smirked inwardly-was he an amorous sap? The thought was slightly unnerving and so he settled for lustful cad, as she had referred him.

The hour grew late and the hall was all but deserted aside from one. Curran's gray eyes leveled on the fire burning low within the hearth, his thoughts disengaged from the object of his stare as he favored a beaker of ale.

So he was to reside at Linden, all to be under the watchful eye of his legendary brother?

He grimaced at the thought. He may have sworn fealty to William but he had not sworn fealty to Fallon. He was his own man. He had an army. He could and would do as he pleased.

His thoughts shifted to the Saxon woman. He smirked as he brought the beaker to his lips, picturing her fiery tresses and vivid, green eyes, sharp with anger as she had pressed the blade to his throat. Women usually feared him; cowered in his presence but this woman, she was different, a woman worth claiming.

He would have her; though she may be Saxon that just made the challenge all the more interesting, more enticing. It pleased him more to know that Fallon lusted for the Saxon woman and that he would be the first to take her.

The door to the hall opened and Curran's face darkened as he cast hooded eyes on his brother.

Fallon crossed the room to stand before Curran, the fire's dim radiance reflected in his amber eyes as they settled grimly on the large shape slouched in the chair.

"You are going to have to learn to quell these mishaps of yours, Curran." Fallon said darkly, "Because you are my brother, 'tis that reason alone that has you unscathed from my temper. I will not have another happening occur such as the one today. My tenants do not agree with me as it is, so for you to reprimand them without my consent will not be tolerated, is that understood?"

Curran slowly gathered to his feet, draining the last of the beaker's contents before slamming it down on the wooden table. He turned sharp, gray eyes on Fallon.

"We may share the blood of the same man, but that does not mean I claim you as my brother. You seem to forget that I was sired from a woman branded non-other than a whore."

The muscle at Fallon's jaw tightened with growing irrita-tion. Curran was clearly goading him and he knew better than to fall prey to his taunting. Curran had a many underlining issues and it was because of these issues that prompted his lenience when it came to brother's mishaps.

But there was only so much he was going to tolerate. He was Lord of Linden and Curran, kin or not, was going to learn his place.

His nostrils flared with his restrained temper. "William has asked me to control your rash behavior, if you cannot learn to limit your actions than you will leave me no choice than to let our King disparage you of it.

Curran's gray eyes narrowed icily, flaring brilliant silver from the anger within. "You need not remind me of your duties in overseeing your reckless brother." He growled with contempt as he swept by Fallon.

Fallon's hand snaked out and seized Curran's arm, turning him about. "Curran-" he said calmly, attempting to rational-ize. "-I am your last resort. You do not realize where you stand with William. He has a great deal of animosity on his plate; the last thing he needs is a Norman under his com-mand terrorizing his people. There are many that seek to rise against him."

Curran smirked, "I am the least of his worries, of that, I can ensure you."

Fallon's brows furrowed, "What do you say?"

Curran hesitated, "There has been talk of treason."

"How do you know this?"

His grin widened, "You wish to put a damper on my rash behavior, but 'tis my behavior that obtains this information. You think I raid the lands for sport? That is where you are wrong."

Fallon's face darkened considerably with rage and uncertainty. "If you are involved-"

Curran wrenched his arm free of Fallon's. "Don't be absurd, brother. You may think me impulsive, but I'm no fool to commit treason." With that he stalked towards the door. He paused with his hand on the latch to peer back at Fallon. "Do you think William will agree with you bedding a Saxon thrall when you are betrothed to the McLeod wench?" his mouth curved into a grin as he jerked the door wide and sauntered from the hall.

Fallon stared after him. Damnation. He had not given any thought to the McLeod woman since Alana or his arranged marriage.

Exhaling sharply, he swept an unsteady hand through his tousled, gold mane. He regained the empty seat before the dim-lit fire and peered longingly into the flames.

At that moment, he would have liked nothing more than to seek the comforts of ale and drain all his quandaries to the bottom of a goblet.

He was to marry the McLeod wench, not to mention, acquaint himself better with the lass before his arranged marriage. How was he to manage that with Alana under the same roof? Aside from that notion, he had a matter far more worrisome. His brother could very well be involved in treason, and that did not settle well with him.

Chapter 17

Alana slept very little throughout the night. She worried for Nettie and what would become of her cousin in the hands of Normans. She envisioned, countless times over in her mind, the day Normans, the same Normans had attacked her village and she came upon Nettie nearly destroyed.

These images plagued her throughout the night and kept slumber at bay. When she did sleep, she did so restlessly, disarranging the thick coverlets on her surprisingly comforting bed.

Fallon had placed her, to her surprise, in what appeared, a suitable guest chamber. The chamber was of adequate size with newly purchased furniture, for she noticed not a speck of dust blemished the smooth, mahogany surfaces.

The bed was fit for a man of extreme size. Sheer drapes enclosed the four-poster bed were now drawn aside to reveal a thick, plush mattress and over-stuffed pillows.

Her amazement at her lavished enclosure was short-lived. She was a prisoner and should think of only escaping. She had once made the mistake of not putting others before herself and because of that grave error, her village was gone and people she had loved were now dead; dead because of Fallon.

With a renewed anger, she paced the chamber, waiting anxiously for her captor. She was finding it difficult to keep her anger at bay for though Fallon had broken his vow in keeping her village safe, his demeanor foretold of tenderness beneath his golden exterior-she shook her head to dismiss the notion.

What was she thinking? He was a Norman. His army had attacked her village. He was called 'The Fury' for an adamant reason. Could he truly be the unyielding savage possessing a rage so destructible that he quelled thousands on the battle field with his mighty sword?

She shivered at the thought. She did not want to think of war.

She sank onto the bed and stared vacantly across the room. Her stomach grumbled hungrily. It was well past dawn and she was beginning to feel a slight anxiety build. Was she to remain in this gilded room for long?

As if on queue, she detected the heavy fall of a man's approach from the outside of her door.

She gathered to her full height and leveled her gaze patiently on the large door. She was oddly deterred by the wild, thumping of her heart and attempted to bring a steady breath into her lungs. Why was she suddenly so unnerved?

And she knew in that moment, when the latch lifted and the door swung wide, producing the object of her uneasiness.

Immediately her pulse quickened and she felt a slight weakening in her knees. She had never seen a man more handsome, more powering than the towering, golden Norman standing before her. She wanted to hate him but strangely, her heart yearned for something unknown but something she was not sure she was ready to acknowledge.

She watched him through narrowed eyes as he slowly closed the door behind him. When he turned back around, he merely stared at her with those burning, amber eyes. She grew uneasy beneath his bold, golden stare and slowly felt her bravado waning.

"Why do you stare at me so?" she demanded, clearly annoyed and uncertain of his manner.

His amber eyes remained fixated on her as he crossed his swarthy arms against the wide expanse of his chest and leaned back against the door. "I find pleasure in looking at you, Alana." The deep lilt of his voice jolted her heart against her breast.

She was finding it difficult to keep her uneasiness at bay. "I would rather you didn't." she snapped, jerking her chin upward.

His mouth curled into a roguish grin, his amber eyes taking on a mischievous gleam. "This displeases you?"

"Greatly."

She felt a subtle jolt as a deep rumble of laughter rose up from his throat. His arms fell away from his chest and he pushed away from the door. He moved towards her and she was startled when her feet carried her backward. Realizing she was retreating, she froze and jerked her head upward to face him squarely.

She felt the air rush from her lungs as he planted his muscled frame firmly in front of her, his thick chest a mere breath apart as she peered with uncertainty into his aureate stare. She felt as though she could lose herself in those eyes. They were so unusual in the way they glinted like the sun but beneath the beauty, was a man known for dangerous and unpredictable tendencies. He could not be trusted.

Those gold eyes swept curiously over her face, "What has changed your opinion of me, Alana?" his voice was surprisingly soft.

She felt her anger stirring. "You are Norman. That reason will suffice."

He fell silent, his eyes taking on that sharp, tawny glint. He was studying her, as if trying to fathom her hatred. Surely he knew the reasons for her anger? The fact that he would act naïve to it only infuriated her more.

"Something has changed in you, fiery one."

"If this displeases you, milord, than I shall see to devoting all my attention to those characteristics." She replied sharply, her voice laced with contempt.

Alana had anticipated his anger, instead, his beautifully sculpted mouth stretched into a devilish grin. "On the contrary, my Saxon beauty, I find your sharp tongue intriguing and quite rousing."

Her eyes widened at his brazen words and she felt her cheeks burn red. Clearing her throat, she took an involuntary step backward. The heat of his muscled frame was unraveling her composure and doing strange, wondrous things to her. She couldn't seem to think clearly with him standing so close.

"You try even now to defy me-" he started huskily, stepping toward her, "-but what you don't know is that your defiance stirs me-" he paused as he reached out and took a thick strand of red hair into his hand.

Alana's throat convulsed at seeing her hair ensnared within his large, callused palm. He toyed playfully with the strand between his forefinger and thumb. She stood frozen, her eyes widening as he twisted his hand, wrapping his wrist around more of her reddened tresses. When she realized his intent, he had already wrapped a significant portion of her hair around his forearm, reeling her close.

When she made a move to jerk away, he yanked gently, pulling her against him. A band of muscle secured itself around her back, pushing her flush against his hardened male body. She yelped at the unexpected proximity of closeness and warmth and squirmed in an attempt to escape his grasp but to no prevail.

He reached up with his free hand and gripped her chin gently, forcing her to peer at him. "You can play the fiery temptress or the gentle maiden, Alana, either way; I will want you just the same."

His arm around her waist tightened, crushing her against him as he captured her lips with unyielding hunger. She struggled beneath the smoldering pressure of his tantalizing mouth but just as quickly as her protests arose, they died within her throat as he deepened the kiss, possessing her with a fierceness that awakened her senses.

Every fiber in her being wanted his kiss, yearned for it, demanded she kiss him back and explore the passions that stirred her traitorous body, but she feared the aftermath, the uncertainty of these waking desires and what they could potentially do to her heart.

With that, she broke away from him.

Fallon pressed his fists to his sides, struggling to maintain the raging hungers that burned in his belly and worse yet, in his groin.

He was a man quite adapt at lovemaking and would recognize desire in the eyes of another. Though she tried so hard to deny him, to hate him, he had caught a flicker of desire in her green eyes, a desire that could match his own.

Damnation. He had made an oath that he would not take her unless willing but he was finding it extremely difficult to ignore the maddening hunger that seem to intensify with her, and it was only her second day at Linden.

He should not have brought her here. It will only cause him great discomfort in all aspects but she was beauty in a world filled of war. She did unnatural things to his heart, things he had never felt.

Aye, he wanted her body, that was evident from the obvious thickening of his manhood, but he wanted more from her, things he had never wanted from countless women he had bedded. He wanted to know everything about her from her childhood up until the present. He wanted to unravel the mystery that surrounded her. He wanted to make her laugh, make her smile and bring light to her green eyes. He wanted to kiss her breathlessly and cradle her at night in his arms while they slept. He wanted to do all these things, but first, he had to break the wall that separated them.

His resolve hardened as his amber eyes leveled sharply on her. "You will do one of two things-" he started, "-you will earn your keep here. I purchased you from Lechmere, which officially makes you mine-" Alana was quick to note that he emphasized the word, "-you may work as a thrall, do tasks and chores about the keep as do the others-" he fell silent to let his words linger.

Alana lifted her chin and asked, "And my other option?"

She noticed his face darkened with yearning, his eyes flaring that brilliant, kindled gold as he took a step toward her. "If you choose to not labor as the others, than you have no choice but to serve me-in my bed."   Her green eyes rounded with- he was certain, anger and a slight stirring beneath her vexation. He grinned inwardly. It would take some time, but he would seduce her into his bed, it was only a matter of time.

Her spine rigid straight and her green eyes flashing daggers, she replied with determined defiance, "I hate to disappoint you, Norman, but I am quite accustomed to tedious labor for the latter of the two is quite revolting to contemplate. I'll gladly manage any task you bestow me."

He resisted another grin, her defiance as clear as his disappointment but he would not be deterred.

He nodded with a teasing grin forming his lips. "Vera' well, fiery maiden. I shall look forward to overseeing all your upcoming tasks."

He could feel her eyes boring into his back as he started for the door. He paused halfway and turned back to her. "If you cannot complete these tasks-" he started, his mouth widening with hopeful intent, "-than I shall see to ensuring the alternative."

Her eyes blazed heatedly, "Not without difficulty, Norman."

His wicked smile only provoked her more. "Try as you might defy me, Alana, but this is a game I look forward too." With that, he left her fuming, making her suddenly aware that she had unknowingly planted herself in his entrapment.

Chapter 18

Alana was still fuming after Fallon had long left the room. She could still feel the heat of his muscled frame and feel his presence as if he were still in the room.

How dare him! She seethed silently. No matter his plans for her, she intended to stay out of his bed, of that she was certain.

He expected her to submit to becoming his thrall? He was in for a surprise for she had little intention of doing so. When the opportune moment presented itself, she and Nettie would flee at first chance.

She struggled to believe she too would become a prisoner of Normans, as the conquered land.

Squaring her shoulders and straightening her spine, she smoothed her wrinkled skirts and started for the door but as she reached for the latch, a persistent knock sounded from the other side.

"Are you in there, girl?" the voice from the other side demanded.

Stepping back, Alana reached out and opened the door. The voice belonged to an older, stout woman with a thick mop of black hair streaked with wisps of silver.

The older woman's face pinched grim and her dark eyes studied Alana with open scrutiny. "You the lass brought from Lechmere?"

Alana was silent a moment as the woman continued to regard her coldly. She lifted her chin, mirroring the older woman's glower, "I am."

The woman's dark eyes narrowed, "I am Matilda and I'll be overseeing your labor-" she paused briefly before adding, "-and I don't tolerate any haughtiness, especially from a Saxon miss."

She stepped aside and motioned Alana onward. "Come along, there is much to be done."

Deciding it was best not to argue; Alana gathered her skirts and followed the austere woman. She wouldn't have to tolerate this Matilda or Fallon for long so it would be in her best interest to comply for the time being.

As Matilda began reciting the daily tasks, Alana followed, assessing the corridors and doorways, planting mental images that could potentially assist her in escaping.

"Are you daft, girl?"

Alana jolted and peered questionably at Matilda, "I'm sorry?"

Matilda's dark eyes narrowed irritably. "You best pay attention, girl, for if you lack in your tasks, Master Fallon will have my hide!"

Alana stiffened, "He is cruel to you?"

Matilda hesitated, as if weighing Alana's concern.

"Master Fallon is a man of extreme temper. Many seek to avoid provoking him. You should heed my warning and do the same." With that the plump woman spun about and proceeded down the hall.

"You will learn to do as the others-churn butter, scrub the floors, weave and if Master Fallon sees fit-" she paused to turn back around to Alana, "-satisfy him."

Alana froze with sudden fury. "I will do nothing of the sort!" she snapped.

Matilda merely peered at her with indifference. "Well now, that is not up to you, is it?" she didn't wait for Alana to respond and turned away.

Glaring at the older woman's back, she slowly fell into pace with Matilda's strides. As they continued down the hall, the distinct clank of steel against steel brought her before a narrow window.

Her blood hastened through her veins at the sight that greeted her. Below the window, Norman soldiers dotted the field, some equipped in armor, and others meagerly dressed in tunics without the protection of chain mail. Several stood aside, studying the strategies demonstrated, those partici-pating in the training wielded deadly weapons ranging from swords, axes and spears.

Most of the men contended on foot while a selected few attempted combat atop their horses.

Alana watched completely enthralled, drawn to their lithe movements and sleek agility in wielding such dangerous weaponry when a cloud drifted astray and sunlight captured a tawny head.

She inhaled a tiny breath as her eyes fell on Fallon. He was not the largest man in the swarm of swarthy bodies, nor the smallest, but something about him had her completely captivated.

He stood beneath the sun bare-chested, the sunlight glinting sharply upon his sleek chest, each muscle protruding with his efforts as he handled the sword with ease, severing the air with fleeting exactness as his men looked on.

She forgot Matilda at her back as she watched his steps, swift and artful as he spun about, stirring the earth with his fluid movements.

There was a slight commotion and the crowd parted, lowering his sword, Fallon peered around as Curran stepped into the clearing. Alana watched from above, intrigued as the two of them exchanged words.

She sensed a moment of hesitation from Fallon and than he extended his arms, motioning the crowd back.

"Come girl-" Matilda called from behind but Alana was far too interested in the activity bellow to pay heed to the older woman.

The men formed a circle and Alana realized Fallon intended to battle his brother. She leaned further out the window as a sword was passed to Curran.

Fallon's face was expressionless but Alana sensed his agitation as he gripped the golden hilt of his sword in a firm, unyielding grasp.

Curran handled his sword lightly, tossing the weapon from palm to palm with a swaggering grin as he advanced left, Fallon stepping right.

The two brothers lifted their swords, the midday sun shimmering against the steel as Curran was the first to strike.

Alana held her breath as she watched Fallon intercept blow by blow, every attempt by Curran was thwarted effortlessly.

She felt the tension beginning to rise even from her stance as Curran's face reddened when Fallon showed little signs of tiring beneath his advances.

Curran veered right and Fallon readily shifted left, raising his sword to deflect the blade that became precariously close to his chest, but Fallon appeared unfazed as he continued to hinder Curran's attacks.

The men surrounding began to shout and applaud, some cheering in mirth for their Chieftain, others encouraging the younger of the two. But praises for his older brother only incited Curran's anger, making him brash and his steps inept.

He wheeled about and whipped his sword in a severing motion, catching Fallon unaware as the tip of the blade grazed his chest. Their was a collected gasp from the men surveying and Alana watched in shock, surprised that Curran would go so far as to wound his brother.

She sensed the sudden rage in Fallon and knew he had kept his skill at bay to keep from harming his younger brother but a maddened frenzy seem to unravel his defenses and he surged without warning.

Curran lifted his blade to shield the unswayable force barreling down upon him. The amused grin swiped clean from his face, he retreated to deflect the relentless crack of steel that caused his weapon to tremble in his hands. He weakened beneath Fallon's maddening blows and his meager attempt to ward Fallon's blade only angered him more.

Alana was disgusted by their show of arrogance to out due one another. She had seen enough. Even if these men were her enemy, violence was senseless; she would not abide this display of masochism all for the sake of who was the better barbarian.

She turned away from the window and started angrily down the corridor, a huffish Matilda following at her heels.

When she reached the yard, she gripped her skirts and started into a run with little heed to the horde of Normans crowding the two.

With as much muster, Alana shoved her way through the muscled bodies until she reached the clearing. Undaunted by the men suddenly aware of her presence, she released a shrill shout laced with anger.

"Cease!"

A gasping Matilda stood to the side, taken aback by the unexpected stillness. Her chieftain no longer entertained the fight; his face impassive as his gold eyes settled on the Saxon woman. Matilda was even more amazed that this mere woman could have the power to still both blades for even the younger of the two Macaulay brothers appeared transfixed.

"This is foolishness!" the girl shouted and Matilda peered fleetingly around the crowd, certain she would be repri- manded for her brazenness but amazingly, the men appeared just as bewildered as she and with that, the Saxon girl spun around and stalked away, all eyes on her retreating back.

Chapter 19

As Alana returned inside, she released the breath she had been holding. Mayhap, she wondered fretfully, she had overstepped her limitations. What had prompted such a reaction from her? Why did it matter to her if these men marred each other with swords?

She knew her reasons though she'd rather not acknowledge them. Closing her eyes she took a moment to steady her breath. Violence was senseless, a picture that rushed to mind, was so quick to remind her so. She was frozen in that nightmare, the lives of so many taken tragically.

"Stupid girl!" Alana whirled around, startled, as an angry Matilda stormed into the hall, wagging a finger in her face. "Do you realize what you have done? No thrall has ever dared to behave in such a manner! I will not have it, do you hear? I will not be accountable because of a Saxon miss whose brain is addled! You will learn your place. You-"

"Silence, haggard!" both women stiffened as a man's voice penetrated the corridor.

Immediately the older woman withdrew and curtsied to the man standing in the shadows. "My apologies, Master Curran-" Matilda straightened and began backing away as Curran stepped into the light, his gray eyes peering coldly at the older woman, who appeared genuinely fearful of the man.

"You are dismissed." He said and Matilda immediately hastened to escape his presence.

Feeling very much cornered and suddenly wary of the warrior, Alana attempted to do the same but as sly as the wolf he resembled, he captured her arm with striking adeptness.

Those gray eyes seem to transform in the light, flaring extraordinary silver. "You have no need to run." He said softly with a tone that lacked gentleness. "I would have a word with you."

Alana studied him in silent, slightly taken aback. If not for his known dealings in cruelty, she would have considered him remarkably handsome, but his certain merciless nature diverted her opinion.

"I have no interest in anything you have to say, Norman." She tried pulling free but his grip stayed her efforts.

He grinned a wolfish grin, "My brother is quite taken with you." Reluctantly he released his grip and stepped around her, his silver eyes drawn to her mouth. "He is not usually affronted with rejection-" he chuckled deeply, "-you are a conquest he seeks to conquer."

Her temper flaring she turned to face him. "I will not be a triumph!"

He stepped toward her and she found herself retreating despite her determination to stand her ground. His silver eyes swept over her frame in a heated stroke. "My brother is not the only man that wishes to conquer you, Saxon."

Green eyes narrowed sharply, "Not ever, Norman."

He stepped toward her and Alana flinched, prompting a crooked smile that curved his cruel lips but any retort was left unsaid as a large, menacing shadow appeared in the hall.

Alana stiffened as her eyes shifted to Fallon. He appeared angry.

"Is their something you need from the Lady, brother?" he growled ominously as he came to stand between them, gold eyes burning into a pair of cold gray ones.

Curran's grin widened, "I was merely asking for the Lady's assistance, she is a healer is she not?"

Fallon accessed him with suspicion. "You have sufficed worse."

Silver eyes shifted past Fallon's shoulder. "Mayhap it pleases me to have the Lady tend my wounds."

"Find another." Fallon hissed as he grasped Alana's arm and started down the hall, pulling her along.

Alana spared a glance over her shoulder and was unnerved by Curran's dark expression. When they turned the corner and lost sight of him, Alana couldn't help but feel slightly relieved and comforted by Fallon's presence.

Peering up at Fallon, she noticed the tension in his jaw, felt the anger in his grip and formidable stance.

When they reached her room, he released her and she backed away, rubbing at her arm where his fingers had been.

She studied him as he crossed the room, his anger seeping from his livid frame.

She was unsure, but she sensed his anger was directed more so at Curran than herself. "You are angry with him."

"Aye." It had not been a question but he seemed compelled to reply.

"He provokes you." She stepped toward him, noticing the distinct tautness of his shoulders. "You would fight him like that?"

He turned around to peer at her, "If I am challenged, I have no other choice but to accept."

"Even your brother?"

"My brother is a fool." Fallon snapped. "I merely accepted to teach him a lesson."

"Why does he challenge you?"

"Why would any man challenge another?" he said, "He is envious."

"But he is your brother-"

"Half-brother." He cut in, "His mother had been a slave from a neighboring village."

Alana stepped forward, "What happened to his mother?"

Fallon stared at the wall with a distant look. "I know little of the woman. My brother does not speak of her or of her whereabouts."

Alan's heart tightened, "Does it not pain him?"

"I wouldn't know." Fallon replied flatly. "Curran is a man of many secrets unbeknownst to me. He confides in no one."

She reached out and gingerly touched his shoulder. He turned to face her and she was captured in his golden stare. "And you, Norman, do you have secrets?"

A grin tugged at the corners of his mouth. "You wish to unravel me, fiery one?"

"I wish to know the man beneath the mask called 'The Fury'." Even after she said the words, she knew she meant them, truly wanted to understand this man that many feared, this warrior whom she seemed undeniably drawn too.

His amber eyes moved over her face, studying her intently. "There is a price."

She stiffened and stepped away from him and was startled when he released a deep rumble of laughter. "Are you amused, Norman?" she snapped irritably.

"Aye, sweet lass." His gold eyes twinkled with mirth as he stepped around her, "You must learn to smile. It does wonders for your beauty."

"You expect me to smile when you suggest compensation in exchange for my inquisitiveness?"

He chuckled, "I am merely teasing you, Alana."

She studied him narrowly, "I know how to laugh." She snapped. "I don't need a Norman to tell me I can't."

"I never said-"

"Oh, bother!" she flounced away from him, clearly vexed.

"Alana!" he rushed for her but was overcome with a fit of laughter, further riling her.

She rounded on him, fists curled, face flushed as she yelled, "Arrogant cad! I'm glad I amuse you!" she pummeled his chest and was satisfied by its solidness. "You pompous brute!"

His laughter filled the room and Alana, despite her best efforts, was smiling as he ducked her flailing fists. "You forget 'Norman pig'!"

"Ah!" she struck aimlessly at his head and he effortlessly tucked and rolled, his forearm encasing her waist, pulling her in momentum to the floor.

Her head rested gently against his forearm and he kept his weight from crushing her as their laughter genially merged, kindling a spark of awareness and a rush of warmth that flowed pleasantly through their embraced bodies.

Her laughter died in her throat as she stared into those liquid gold eyes. He stared at her as if sunlight flowed in the iris of his eyes. He took the breath from her lungs with the slightest touch. Each breath hindered with his closeness.

She knew the moment he would kiss her. Her body craved his touch, yearned for his kiss. He captured her lips with sweet gentleness. She was pleasantly surprised and yet, she knew this man existed beneath the one called 'The Fury'. His hands pulled gently at her fiery strands; his fingers trailing the length of her tresses as he favored her with soft kisses.

She arched against him, reveling in the solid length of him stretched above her. She was willing to give herself into the fervent desires incited by each touch and his every caress. She wanted to explore the wondrous things he roused in her. She wanted to forget for a moment that he was her enemy, her captor. Alana believed she would have given herself to him if not for the sudden pounding on the chamber door.

Just like that. The fire diminished.

She knew her face was reddened and she made an attempt to right her hair. The pounding persisted at the door and by the vexed look on Fallon's face; he was clearly not pleased with the interruption.

Alana however, took it as a foretoken. Even now her body still craved for something that only Fallon could appease and the thought made her blush clear to her toes. She was a clever and intelligent woman, but when it came to desires shared between a man and a woman, she was as naïve as they come.

She turned her back to the door as Fallon jerked it open with enough force to startle the messenger in the hall. "What is it?" he growled to the man on the other side.

"Beg your pardon, milord-" spoke the little man outside the door, "-a visitor has arrived at Linden."

Fallon frowned, "I received no missive-"

"She claims she is your betrothed, milord."

Chapter 20

Alana felt as if she had been doused in cold water. Every exhilarating emotion that had flowed through her body a moment ago had all but dissolved like mist.

She stared questionably at Fallon whose body was as rigid as stone. He appeared angry and avoided her all together. He mumbled something to the man on the other side and than slowly closed the door.

Feeling quite the fool, Alana turned away the moment their eyes would have connected. How should she feel? She wondered confusingly. Should she be angry or relieved? She realized she had no right to be angry. She would have given herself freely to this Norman if not for the sudden circumstances. She decided that it was in her best interest. She had vowed that she would not submit to his advances and just like that, she had nearly crumbled under her defenses. Was she that naïve to his desires?

She felt his eyes upon her but what was there to say?

"Alana-"

Despite her best efforts to forget the passions sparked between them, she couldn't help but feel slightly hurt. She turned around and met those amber eyes. Lifting her chin, she asked with an unfeeling tone, "Is there ought I to can do for you, milord?"

Her impassive manner did not go unaware and his demeanor quickly hardened. He sensed the change in her and was displeased but Alana no longer cared. She had forgotten her most essential priority; escaping Linden, and now that Fallon had a distraction, escape would seem achievable.

"Nay." He replied darkly, studying her intensely with his gold eyes.

She nodded curtly and left the room.

Fallon stalked angrily to the great hall, his mood black as he stormed through the corridors. The image of Alana in his arms stilled burned heavily in his mind as well as her blank expression when she had left the chamber.

He had struggled to lower what defenses he had and in a split second, her barriers were replaced, blocking him entry.

He was in a foul mood and had little intention of making his betroth comfortable. The woman had no right showing up unintended without his knowledge. He could wring the McLeod's neck with his hands for this interference!

When he reached the great hall, he shoved the doors wide enough to crash loudly against the opposing walls, startling the woman standing amidst the dais. Seeing the McLeod woman standing so formally within his hall irked his nerves and she was not alone.

His anger growing, Fallon surveyed the number of men aligned along the wall, taking note that all were armed and equipped in battle armor.

Raising a golden brow, he cast a dark glare on his betroth. "Is there a reason these men have come armed, milady?"

The small woman stepped forward, her dark eyes doing a slow leisure of his frame as she came to stand before him. "These are my father's men." She spoke gently, her voice strong and feminine. "They accompanied me to Linden to ensure my safety since my future husband had not returned for me."

His eyes narrowed shrewdly. "You should not have come without my knowledge." He growled, "I would have sent word when the time was at hand for your arrival. You coming unaware have displeased me."

"Forgive me, milord, 'twas not my decision but my father's. He believed I would have been far safer in your hands."

Fallon groaned inwardly. McLeod merely wanted to ensure the safety of his lands and was attempting to hurry their union along. "Well than you may send word to your father that I have every reason to see you safely back home." He turned around but a strong male voice stopped his flight.

"That cannot happen, Macaulay."

Fallon paused and slowly turned to the guttural voice that had spoken. The man standing at his betrothed's side resembled her in striking resemblance. He was exceptionally tall, built in lean muscle with hair as black as coal. He had the same unusual sloe eyes but a far more demanding presence than his betroth.

Fallon stepped toward the man in sudden pique. "Who are you to dispute my word in my hall?"

The man appeared undaunted as his chin jutted upward in open defiance. "I am Alec McLeod, brother to your betrothed."

Fallon smirked, "Brother? Your father had not mentioned a son. What did he think to gain by sending you here, lad?"

The man, who clearly was not a youth, narrowed his eyes sharply on Fallon. "My father has reason to believe that you intend to break your oath-"

"You question my loyalty to my King!" Fallon snapped, moving forward in several angry strides.

His betrothed winced beneath his unveiled rage and edged closer to her brother. Alec however remained unaffected, sizing Fallon as if considering drawing his sword.

"Understand this, Saxon-" Fallon growled, "-William is foremost my King. I gave him my word and I intend to keep it."

In the silence that followed, the two doors from behind opened and all eyes drew to the man that entered some even took an involuntary step backward. "Have you a need of me, milord?" Ranulf's voice resonated sharply in the room.

Fallon straightened, "Nay Ranulf, 'tis naught but a misunderstanding." He turned away, "See that my betrothed and her brother are seen to their horses."

"Wait!"

Inhaling deeply through his nose, Fallon turned not to the man, but to his betrothed who had spoken out.

The woman who was to be his wife was a comely sort but her alluring features, that would have stirred many, did naught for him. "Aye?" he asked with seldom tolerance.

Her uneasiness of him was quite clear as she reluctantly stepped toward him but her intrigue was far greater. "The King has informed us that you were given leniency in time so that you and I may get better acquainted. How is that to be accomplished if you cast us out?"

Fallon clenched his jaw until the muscle there began to pulse. "I am Lord here. I have the right to cast out anyone if it pleases me. You, milady, are no exception."

"What if I went to the King?" she challenged, "What if I went to William and said that you refused me? Do you think he would be pleased to know that you have not attempted to make an effort?"

Fallon studied the woman in seething silence. He gritted his teeth to keep from lashing out at the woman who was to be his wife. He sensed her fear but detected her urgency and an eagerness to have a husband and wondered questionably at that.

"Ranulf-" he turned to his man, "Have a servant accompany my betrothed to a room and see that her men are given suitable accommodations." With that he spun around and departed the hall, leaving his betrothed glaring crossly at his back.

"He is an overbearing brute!" Lady Rosalind mumbled crisply to her maid who trailed meekly at her heels.

Once secured in her guest chamber, she unclasped her cloak and handed it to Morag and did a perceptive study of her room. She was not pleased. She was a daughter of a wealthy man and was accustomed to the lavished commodities that life had to offer.

The chamber lacked extravagance and luxury. No matter. She thought considerably. That would all change once she was mistress of Linden.

Smiling to herself, she circled the room and imagined its potential. Her heart fluttered at the thought, and her thoughts shifted to her husband-to-be.

He was indeed the epitome of the tales foretold and she certainly feared the man but that had not swayed her. She prided herself for her cleverness and knew this would benefit her greatly. When she first heard of her arranged marriage to the formidable warrior, she had been outraged and furious with her father, certain it was all for personal gain, but when she had set eyes on Fallon 'The Fury', she knew no other man would compare.

When she had learned of William's invasion, she feared of being cast out like all the others. She had not been raised to become a slave! Though she did not approve of her new king, she knew that marrying Fallon Macaulay would be her wisest of decisions.

With this union, she would maintain her position and gain the respect from those who had conquered her land. She would not have to fear them; instead, they would curtsy to her because she would be wife to the most feared and respected warrior under William's command.

It was an honorable match. Her father combined with the sanction of Fallon's clan would be a force to reckon with.

She settled comfortably onto the drab coverlet that covered the bed and peered dreamily up at the ceiling. She would bare him many children, she thought with a smile curving her lips. She imagined her children with the same untamed golden mane and eyes that brilliant shade of sun.

Aye, she was particularly pleased with her husband-to-be. She was slightly concerned that he appeared unmoved by her beauty. Most men scrambled for her affections. It mattered not. She had yet to meet a man that was aloof to her charms and Fallon would be no exception.

He needed time to accept their union.

Chapter 21

The great hall was humming with life as the hour grew well into the evening. The servants were now well aware of the unexpected arrival of their Master's betrothed and seemingly surprised.

The warriors crowding the trestle table sipped at hearty goblets of mead and ale while feasting on salted haddock and maize corn. They conversed informally amongst one another, as they indulged their hungers, with little talk of war focusing solely on gaiety.

Lynette lingered in the shadows of the hall as all else carried on about her. From beneath hooded eyes she surveyed the men aligned along the table.

She shivered inwardly as her eyes settled on the badly scarred warrior. His plate remained untouched and he entertained naught but his ale. The women in the room seem to shrink away from the giant in fear but the warrior seemed unperturbed.

Her eyes passed briefly over the man called Ivan whose laughter carried the loudest amongst the hall as he playfully snatched a chunk of haddock from the man's plate sitting across from him.

The Norman whose haddock was seized released a rumble of laughter as he slapped the fish from Ivan's hand, his russet beard jutting beneath his bulbous nose.

But it was neither of these men that had caught her attention. One warrior in particular sat amongst the crowd, immersing himself in the meal and the entertainment.

Her eyes settled on the one called Gavin whose eyes trailed wickedly over a serving wench. A swift and unexpected pang of jealousy gripped her but just as abruptly as the emotion surfaced, she shoved it away. She was startled by this and equally shocked by her reaction.

Gavin should be of no interest to her but she couldn't help but notice how the women in the room seemed drawn to him. Aye, she could admit even to herself that he was the most attractive man she had ever seen but he was a Norman and an arrogant one at that! Even now he flirted openly with the women around him, flashing smiles and even having the audacity to wink at another.

He appeared quite comfortable with all the women practically swooning at his feet, brandishing him with timid glances and soft giggles. Her ears seemed to burn with his sultry voice as it passed in the room as he lavished the women with compliments that catered to their obvious charms.

Lynette was absolutely irritated by the sight and had an intriguing thought of dumping her tray of ale onto the rogue's lap.

As she started from the shadows, she stopped even before she stepped as the doors opened followed by an immediate hush as a dark-haired woman entered the hall.

Alana had done her best to avoid the hall. She could hear the commotion, surely for the arrival of their chieftain's bride, and sought to escape the festivity.

She was hopelessly and profoundly confused by her feelings for Fallon and was shocked by her feeble barriers to keep him at bay.

How could she forget her villagers and the village he burned? How could she forget that day she had nursed him back to health only to have his men attack Nettie?

These afterthoughts restored her anger.

His bride had no sooner arrived at the best of times. Mayhap Fallon would now seek the company of his betrothed and leave her in peace.

She knew Nettie was in the hall and she had not seen her cousin since their arrival at Linden and wanted desperately to speak with her but a nagging feeling stayed her.

She wanted nothing more than to dislodge any emotions that catered to her heart when it came to Fallon but she couldn't ignore the pending thought of coming face-to-face with his betrothed.

With that in mind, she decided to retire for the evening. As she turned around, she was startled to see a man standing across from her, watching her curiously with dark eyes. "I am sorry-" the man said casually, "I did not mean to frighten you."

"Is there something I can get for you, milord?" she had never seen this man before and wondered if he had come with Fallon's betrothed.

He stepped towards her and she retreated and sought the corridor with her eyes. He detected her weariness and reassured quickly, "I mean you no harm."

"Who are you?" she knew she was overstepping her boundaries as a thrall but she was curious about this man who studied her with equal interest.

"My name is Alec McLeod." He curtsied to her and offered a smile that somewhat eased the uneasy feeling in her.

Alana frowned, "You are Saxon?"

He grinned, "I am." He paused as his dark eyes swept over her with sudden eagerness, "As are you?"   She nodded, "If you are Saxon, how do you walk about Linden freely as you do?"

He motioned to the hall past her shoulder, "My sister is to the marry 'The Fury'."

She felt a slight tug on her heart and sought to ignore it. "I see." She paused and than asked, "Have you pledged fealty to your Norman king?"

His dark eyes had a peculiar glimmer in the dimness of the corridor as he studied her. "My father has vowed his allegiance to 'The Conqueror'."

"And you are pleased with the man your sister is to marry?"

He grinned, "I had no say in the matter."

The hall behind her grew boisterous and she knew it was only a matter of time before Fallon would be on his way to join his bride. "I am sorry but I must be along."

He grasped her arm as she swept by him, "What is your name?"

She hesitated, unsure whether she should trust this man but what harm was there in telling him her name? "I am Alana."

He smiled, flashing a row of perfectly white teeth. "You are beautiful, Alana."

"Your flattery is wasted, Saxon-" came a bristling tone from the shadows.

Alana stiffened as Fallon stepped forward, his gold eyes burning hotly on the hand that gripped her arm. "Your compliments fall flat-" Fallon growled as he stepped toward Alec, "-this woman has been promised to another, so you understand any further pursuit is unnecessary?"

Alana was so shocked by the untruth of his words that she had not realized the hand on her arm had fallen and Alec no longer stood at her side.

Alec's expression was taut as he asked, "Should you not be at your bride's side, entertaining her?"

Fallon's face flushed a seething red and Alana envisioned the man from the field, wielding his blade with deadly intent.

Before any of the two men could react, the doors to the hall opened, amplifying the unruly spouts of drunken men.

Alana spied the scarred warrior called Ranulf and knew by the giant's expression that he sensed the tension in the air.

"Have you a need of me, milord?" Alana shivered at the man's gruff, baritone voice.

Fallon was silent a moment as he weighed the man's concern considerably but Alana knew Fallon would need no assistance in severing this man if it pleased him to do so. "Nay, Ranulf." Fallon replied, "We are finished."

Alana watched Alec disappear down the hall but the tension still lingered heavily in the corridor.

Remembering Fallon's deceit, she spun around to face him, "I am promised to another? Lies come so easily to you, Fallon."

"Mayhap I speak truthfully."

Alana stiffened, "You cannot-"

His gold eyes burned heatedly in the dark. "I have that power, Alana, and if you continue to test my tolerance I will have you matched with a Norman of my choosing to ensure your obedience." He hesitated and than said softly, "If you were mine, I would keep you confined from all eyes."

Her heart fluttered at his words but remembering her anger, she inhaled deeply through her nose and replied through clenched teeth, "It is good you are soon to marry, Fallon, because any Norman you choose would be most preferred to you."

Before her heart deceived her, she gathered her skirts and fled the hall as quickly as her steady strides could carry her. She couldn't stand his presence for no more than several moments, for in fear of exposing her heart.

Chapter 22

Rosalind spied her soon-to-be-husband and narrowed her eyes in chagrin as he crossed the hall to where she sat at the head of the trestle table.

She was very displeased; having spent a majority of her evening alone to entertain a hall full of drunken warriors was not how she had anticipated their first afternoon together.

As he settled at her side, she noticed his face was grim and felt the tension pouring from him in waves.

"I had hoped you would join me before the evening was through." She said beneath her breath.

He said naught and as Rosalind spared him a glance, she noticed the muscle at his jaw was taut. "Where have you been?" she questioned, her aggravation growing with his silence.

Her question seemed to spark a response for he turned and cast a sharp glare upon her. "My whereabouts are none of your concern, milady, you will remember hereafter to keep your curiosity at bay."

He turned away from her and Rosalind's mouth fell open with disbelief. No one had ever dared talk to her in such a manner! Remembering there were others watching, she clamped her mouth shut and pasted a smile on her face. It mattered not; once they were married things between them would change.

Was it because she was Saxon? She peered at him beneath her lashes. She knew he had been displeased with their arranged marriage but she believed he would come to terms with it as she had. She was a beautiful woman, of that she was certain, she had many admirers, and her dowry was significant, what man wouldn't want her?

Fallon emptied the last of his mead from his goblet and slammed it on the table. He felt the presence at his side of the woman he was to marry but envisioned a different woman in his head.

When he had come upon Alana and Alec in the corridor, it had angered him beyond reason. Alec was Saxon. Had the two of them been conspiring? Did Alec have a sudden interest in Alana?

The latter of the two chafed his nerves. The idea of Alana with another man riled his blood. He was not pleased that his betrothed was at Linden and further displeased to find Alana and Alec speaking softly in the hall.

Gritting his teeth he thought of nothing more satisfying than teaching Alana a lesson. Mayhap he should follow out on his threats and match her with one of his men?

He peered around the table and his eyes settled on Ivan. Ivan was an awry sort and was not a suitable match for Alana.

His gaze drifted to Ranulf. The giant preferred solitude and would not take kindly to having a woman figuratively chained to his side.

His eyes settled on Gavin and lingered. Gavin would be considerable but his faithfulness was questionable and than he decided against it. Gavin was too much of a libertine to contemplate marrying one woman.

He knew none of the men in the hall would be suitable for Alana because in the back of his mind, he knew, they were not him.

Later that evening, Rosalind was back in her unadorned chamber, still vexed. She was not pleased with how Fallon had treated her. She was to be his wife, she deserved a great deal of respect and he blatantly dismissed her as if she were a lowly peasant.

She knew at dinner, something had been troubling him but what, she knew not.

"Milady?" someone called suddenly from outside her door followed by a persistent knock.

More agitated than before that she had been disturbed, Rosalind gathered to her feet and crossed the room to the door. "What is it?" she demanded.

"Master Fallon has asked that I see to any needs you may have?" the older woman continued.

Rosalind smiled; mayhap her husband-to-be did care for her?

Still smiling, she jerked the door open to peer at the older, ample woman standing on the other side. The servant curtsied and Rosalind wrinkled her nose at the older woman's unkempt hair and disheveled clothes.

"I am Matilda." The woman said sweetly, flashing a crooked grin. "May I assist you, milady?"

Rosalind struggled to conceal her grimace for she'd rather turn the plain woman away but had second thoughts. Mayhap she could pry a little of Fallon from the old woman. She needed an informant; someone willing to spill his secrets.

"Come in please." She stepped aside and motioned the woman forward.

Alana was just settling into bed when a knock came at her door. For some reason, she couldn't help the way her heart battered against her breast.

She peered at the door as if fearful of who lay on the other side until another knock sounded, bringing her to the present.

Clearing her throat, she grabbed a robe and quickly wrapped herself modestly before retrieving the door.

When a large, solid frame greeted her on the other side, she held her breath as her fingers gripped the latch. "The hour is late, milord."

"I would speak with you, Alana." Fallon's voice spoke from the darkness of the corridor.

"Now is not a good time." She attempted to shut the door on him but his boot lodged in the doorway and with an effortless nudge, he pushed the door open and his brawny frame stepped into the room.

Alana swallowed a sudden lump down in her throat as she stepped away from him, gripping the edges of her robe together as he quietly closed the door.

Feeling suddenly very helpless, she retreated another step from him as his amber eyes assessed her frame, making her all the more aware of her barely clad body.

She met his stare boldly, "What do you want, Norman?"

His eyes glinted gold as he peered at her, "You are a servant."

Her eyes narrowed, "You have made my status clear, Norman."

He stepped toward her, "You will cease calling me Norman."

She pushed her chin upward, "Is that not what you are, a Norman?"

His lip curled as if he was going to growl and she almost laughed if not for the sheer size of him that seemed to absorb all the air from the room.

"A servant does not converse in a hall with a complete stranger."

Her temper flaring, Alana stepped toward him until she stood beneath him, her eyes connecting angrily with his. "You insist on convincing me of my station, Norman, but what I don't understand is if I am such a lowly servant, why do I sleep here, in this room as if I were a guest? Should I not be sleeping with the rest of the lowly serfs, in your hall, on a bench?" she demanded.

She could detect the muscle along his jaw pulsating with-whatever emotion he bordered-she was unsure.

His gold eyes moved over her face making her suddenly uneasy.

"Did you mean what you said?" she asked softly, surprising herself that she would speak the words aloud, but she needed to know.

His handsome face furrowed with puzzlement, "What?"

"Do you intend to match me with one of your men?"

He gritted his teeth and inhaled deeply through his nose before responding, "Nay."

"Than why did you threaten me?"

He reached up and slipped his hand around her neck, seizing a fistful of hair, "Because I was mad with jealousy. Is that what you want to hear, Alana? That the very idea of another man touching you drives me to madness?"

He wasn't hurting her, but she felt the strength in his grip as he lightly teased the strands at the nape of her neck. Her eyes settled on his beautifully sculpted mouth and she had a sudden indecent urge to kiss him.

He recognized her hunger and before she could react, his grip tightened and he tugged her forward, crushing her body against him.

At first, she resisted, but she realized she wanted this every bit as he and opened her mouth to his kisses. His hands moved hungrily over her luscious frame, yanking mindfully at her meager robe and tossing it to the floor.

He kissed her with an eagerness that made her heart pound. His hands crushed her thighs to him and she felt his hardness pressing against her, proclaiming his hunger for her. She wanted to give into the desires he stirred in her but a sudden recollection caused her to come to her senses.

She pulled away from him and his arms tightened. He lifted his head to peer down at her. "What is it?" he was breathless.

She shook her head, "Your betrothed."

His face hardened as his arms fell away from her.

Alana peered around and found her discarded robe. She quickly snatched it from the floor and clumsily slipped back into it. "This was a mistake." She said once properly clothed and moved around him to open the door.

His hand lashed out and seized her arm, "This is no folly, Alana." His voice was hard and edged with cruelty. "Betrothed or not, I intend to have you beneath me."

Alana blanched as if she had been slapped. This man was 'The Fury'. Her rejection of him was etched heatedly in his face.

Her anger restored, she wrenched out of his grip. "If I had known you were such a heartless cad, I would have left you in that forest."

His lips curled into a grin, "Nay, if you had known than what you know now, you still would have done what you did. You cannot deny there is a fire between us. You want me as I want you, Alana. No other man such like Alec McLeod or your Rowan, will stir you as I do."

Her heart clenched at the mention of Rowan and without pause, she lifted her hand to smack his roguish face. His fingers seized her wrist and she winced beneath the heat in his gold eyes.

He peered at her with pique, "What has happened to your winsome lad?"

Alana made an effort to kick his shin but he effortlessly dodged her blow. Growing increasingly upset, she attempted to pull free from him.

Fallon was startled by her anger and tears. "Does he seek you as we speak?" he pressed.

"Norman bastard!" she cried, "How can you speak so crudely of a man who lies cold from your blade!"

Chapter 23

Fallon stepped back from her, his face twisting with puzzlement. "What do you say?"

Alana snorted, "Are you feigning ignorance?"

Fallon reached out and gripped her arms, "What are you saying, Alana?"

She frowned for his expression appeared sincere. "Rowan is dead." Her voice trembled, "Your men killed him."

He blanched and his brows drew together with confusion. "My men had no reason to harm him, let alone kill him."

"Your men did more than just kill an innocent man. They burned my village, killed others defending their homes and almost ravished my cousin!"

His fingers tightened around her arms and she flinched beneath the sudden anger burning sharply in his gold eyes. "Alana, my men would not have done these heinous crimes without reason."

Alana studied his face, looking for signs of deception, but he appeared sincere and quite angry of her accusations against his men. "You truly didn't know?"

"How could I have known?"

"That day, at the cottage, you stopped them from harming Nettie?"

His fingers gentled around her arms, "I had given you my oath that no harm would come to you or any of your village; if I had known than what I know now I would have personally sought to punish those responsible."

She peered at him doubtingly, "Why not punish those men now?"

His hands fell away. "What good would it do to punish them now when it is done?"

She felt her anger resurfacing. "That's not good enough." She hissed, "You gave me your word!"

"Alana-" he reached for her and she wrenched away from him. He straightened and inhaled sharply through his nose. "I cannot make amends for what has been done to you but I will see to those who have wronged you."

Her green eyes narrowed angrily, "That sounds to me like a promise." She swept past him and paused by the door. "Do me a favor, Fallon-" she wrenched the door wide and stepped aside and glared at him. "Don't make any more promises that you don't intend to keep."

As the door swung open, a shadow shifted to blend un-detected in the corridor and with hooded eyes, watched as Alana swept down the hall. What was more infuriating was the man that followed, taking a moment to stare longingly at Alana's retreating frame before heading the opposite way.

A grimace curved Curran's lips as he watched Fallon tread the corner.

He stepped from the darkness and turned his head in the direction where Alana had vanished. He had overheard the words exchanged between them, had not mistaken the look in his brother's eyes, a look he thought never to witness on the face of a man claimed to have no heart.

He wondered what Fallon's betroth would think to find her husband-to-be seducing a serf.

He smirked a discerning sneer; having the McLeod wench at Linden may prove useful in his tactics in having Alana all to himself.

With that notion, he sauntered back into the shadows.

The next morning, Rosalind found herself eating breakfast alone. She shoved her plate away in disgust and exhaled a sharp breath.

This was not how she had expected her stay at Linden to go. Her betroth was nowhere to be found when he should be indulging her at every turn. Should he not be showing her the ways of the keep? She was to be the mistress of Linden and with that came many responsibilities that she was eager to take on.

"Good day, milady."

She was startled by the voice that addressed her and even more so by the man who stood before her.

The man had a startling set of gray eyes that seem to reflect a hint of silver. Rosalind found herself drawn to his wickedly dark bearing but she had a slight inkling that this man was trouble.

She raised her nose at him, "Can I do something for you-eh?" she realized he had given no name.

He stepped forward, "My apologies, I am Curran. Fallon's brother."

Rosalind raised a brow at this; her betroth had not mentioned a brother. "You do not look anything like Fallon." She observed.

He smirked, "So they say."

She arose from the table and gathered her skirts. "If you'll excuse me." She had no intention of making conversation with her betrothed's brother.

As she started past him, he said, "I'm surprised my brother did not join you-he is usually not so neglectful of his women." Rosalind gasped at his insensitive remark but realized how she could use this to her advantage. "Your brother-does he have many women?" the thought enraged her.

She stared at his back as he walked to the table and picked at her untouched plate. He turned slightly to peer over his shoulder at her, a slight grin curving his mouth.

"As of late, just one in particular."

She narrowed her eyes in sudden vexation, "Care to specify?"

His grin widened as he popped a grape in his mouth. "A red-haired serf."

Rosalind inhaled sharply through her nose, "You are sure?"

"Aye."

A sudden thought occurred to her and she swept the man with a probing stare. "Why would you tell me this?"

His expression grew stern and he turned to fully face her. "The two of us share one common interest."

She eyed him suspiciously, "And that is?"

He stepped toward her, "You want Fallon-and I want the red-haired serf."

Chapter 24

The next day, Alana buried herself in her tasks, hoping to steal a chance with Nettie to devise an escape.

As she passed in the corridor, she came to the same window overseeing the training field.

The sight of Fallon, his muscles straining beneath the heated sun, his golden tresses teased from his hurried movements and the way his large frame shifted in such an agile way, made her heart flutter uncontrollably.

She gripped the linen in her hands a little more tightly as she watched, completely entranced.

Her heart truly wanted to believe he had nothing to do with the attack on her village, but logic had her thinking otherwise. He was a Norman, and because of that he could not be trusted.

"Something catch your eye, serf?"

Alana gasped as she spun around; startled to come face to face with Fallon's betrothed. Up close, the woman was understandably beautiful, but the scowl that marred her face, put a hindrance on her elite beauty.

Struggling to restrain her temper, she merely shook her head and replied, "Nay, milady." Grasping the linen, she made her way around the woman, feeling suddenly uncomfortable.

"You were brought here against your will?"

Alana paused in the hall and slowly turned to peer at the woman, "Milady?"

Rosalind waved a hand in the air as if to dismiss the question, "What I mean to say is that you have a desire to leave, yes?"

Alana swept the woman with a cautionary perusal. The woman was Saxon, could she be trusted? She was Fallon's betrothed, had he put her up to this?

"You need not say anything for your silence is answering enough."

"You wish to help me?"

She nodded.

Alana frowned, growing more suspicious. "I don't understand."

The woman began walking a circular motion, sweeping Alana with a distasteful inspection from head to toe. "I wish I could tell you it is because we are of the same lineage but sadly for you, that is not the reason."

Alana was taken aback by this, "If not for that reason, than why-"

"You are a distraction." The woman's voice grew distinctly sharp, "It appears that my betrothed fancies you and I cannot have that."

Alana's heart began to race in her chest. How could she have possibly drawn these assumptions when they had been so discreet? She could not even make sense of her own feelings for Fallon or whatever it was that drew her to him, but she wasn't about to tell that to his betrothed.

"I am not an ignorant woman. I know when a man desires a woman." she straightened her shoulders and peered down her nose at Alana. "I can't afford to have some impertinent serf getting in the way of my marriage."

Alana felt her anger rising but was very clear as to the woman's intention. "You plan to help me escape?"

She nodded.

"And my cousin?"

"I never said I would-"

"I won't leave without her." Alana exclaimed.

The woman inhaled through her pert nose and glared at Alana with contempt. "I suppose I can arrange that." She glanced out the window at her betrothed. "Do your best to stay away from him in the meantime, serf." With that she fled before someone spied them.

Alana glanced out the window and felt her heart grow heavy. This was what she had wanted all along but why did it feel so very wrong?

Alana had not anticipated the woman's desperation in having her gone. That evening, she had already arranged a scheme to ensure her escape.

Evidently, she was already in cohorts with one of the servants, who informed her of Fallon's whereabouts, including his men, who at that very moment were absorbing all the mead in the hall.

As she waited, she dealt with a sudden swarm of feelings and thoughts that tied to Fallon and their undeniable attraction. Even if the circumstances had been different between them, the two of them could not be. He had been ordered by his King to marry the McLeod woman, there was no way around that.

Where she waited, a shadow fell in at her side and she nearly jumped out of her skin.

"Alana!"

Alana was overjoyed as she embraced the shadow. "Nettie."

"We don't have time to rejoice." Fallon's betrothed suddenly appeared, pulling them apart and ushering them forward. "I was told there is a hidden door just beyond this hall."

"And from there, than what?" Alana prodded, growing anxious.

"As long as you stick to the passage, it should eventually lead you outside to the wall that has a small opening that you can slip through."

"How do you know all this?" Nettie asked her voice laced with uncertainty.

"Does it matter?" Rosalind bristled. "You need not worry about the guards at the rear; they were slipped some ale and are sleeping as I speak. If you go now, you may not be detected. Once you reach the outer wall. I cannot help you."

Alana straightened as Rosalind turned and fled down the hall, leaving the two of them to their plan.

Nettie turned to Alana in the dark, grasping her arm desperately. "Alana, should we go through with this? What if we get caught?"

"It's now or never, Nettie. We have to try."

Gripping Nettie's arm, Alana tugged her along. Just as the woman had said, their was a hidden door, so perfectly etched into the stone wall, that not even a servant cleaning the stone would have noticed the tiny outline of the door. The two of them pried the door apart and very quietly slipped into another passage that was extremely damp and dark.

Nettie began to whimper fearfully, clutching at her arm, as they trailed the dirt and web invested corridor that seem to carry on with no opening. When they finally broke into the brisk, night air, they heaved a sigh of relief.

Alana scanned the area and sure enough, the guards were slumped at their posts. Catching Nettie's arm, they stumbled upon a breakage in the wall and from their, they slipped into the night.

During his meal, Fallon was aware of one specific absence. His betrothed was no where to be found. Truly, he did not care of the woman's whereabouts, but she was a Saxon, roaming freely about his keep, and that was a disquieting notion.

Draining the last of his ale, he slammed the goblet down and rose from the table. His men carried on with the meal, entertaining the women and mead, but he caught eyes with Ranulf and motioned the giant to him.

"Aye, milord?" Ranulf asked once in the privacy of the corridor.

"It appears my betrothed has gone missing. Will you do me the liberty of finding the woman and bringing her to the hall, I will follow shortly."

Ranulf nodded, "Aye, my liege."

Fallon turned and started in the opposing direction, his betrothed no longer of interest. There was only one woman he wished to see and that woman had managed to avoid him all day.

As he rounded the corner that would eventually lead him to her room, a small shadow collided roughly against him.

Instinctively, his arms came up and wrapped around the feminine frame, crushing her to his chest, but the eyes that met his in the dark were not a brilliant green, but a sooty black.

Almost at once, his arms fell away but his hand seized Rosalind's arm. "What are you doing here?" he demanded, searching her face.

He suspected her of some mischief but her expression revealed naught. "Looking for you, milord." She replied sweetly.

He narrowed his eyes suspiciously, "And you thought to find me here?"

She stared down at the hand clamped tightly around her forearm and he almost thought he heard her throat convulse. "I was told that you wander these halls often. I-I thought you would be here."

He took the explanation for a falsehood, "You didn't think to check the hall first?"   Her lashes fanned her dark eyes as she dropped her head. "I am sorry if I have displeased you."

He knew the wench was lying and he fully intended to find out just what exactly she was hiding. "I think it best you return to the hall."

"Will you come along?" her gentle, enticing voice had little affect on him but her words when first arrived at Linden scraped his thoughts.

"What if I went to William and said that you refused me? Do you think he would be pleased to know that you have not attempted to make an effort?"

He sparred a glance beyond her shoulder to where Alana's door waited and decided he would go to her later. Biting down on a surfacing growl, he seized Rosalind's arm and together they returned to the hall.

"Alana, I'm frightened." Nettie's voice rang through the dark as the two of them pushed there way through shrubbery.

Alana would not reveal to Nettie that she was equally frightened because that would only increase their fears, so with as much bravado as she could muster, she clamped down on her anxiety and turned to console her cousin.

"I'm sure there is a neighboring village nearby where we could rest for the night."

Nettie wrapped herself in her arms and shivered against the nightly chill. "We shouldn't have done this, there are other dangers-"

"Nettie!" Alana spun around but once she saw her cousin's pale face and wide, fearful stare, her anger deflated. "Would you rather we go back and become a Norman's slaves?" She was surprised when Nettie didn't respond.

"Nettie?"

She shrugged, "It wasn't like they mishandled me or treated us poorly?"

Alana shook her head, "You're only saying that because you'd rather be there than out here. You're just frightened."

She turned back around and continued, refusing to dwell on the fact that Nettie was absolutely right. Fallon had not abused them, had not attempted to follow through on his threats-her mind could only replay their kisses shared between them, the memory of his arms secured around her waist, holding her to him, as he kissed her like no other man had ever done.

She shook the images away but couldn't help but wonder if she running from him or the feelings he stirred in her?

Chapter 25

It turned out that there had not been a neighboring village nearby and wouldn't be one for many miles.

Alana and Nettie had made a pallet out of the forest floor and slept restlessly through the night, fearful of what the darkness concealed.

As Alana rose, stretching her limbs, she wondered if Fallon realized they were gone and could he possibly be looking for her now?

Brushing the twigs from her skirt, she gently shook Nettie awake. Her cousin moaned and rolled over, opening her eyes to a stream of sunlight pouring through the canopy above.

"We should get going." Alana said, peering around.

"Why do you sound suddenly nervous?" Nettie asked, sitting up and following Alana's gaze with growing peril.

"I'm not, it's just we've slept long enough and wasted time. Come on." Helping Nettie to her feet, they started back on the trail. Alana realized mayhap this had been a mistake. She had not thought beyond the point of escaping the keep and now that they were far from Linden, she truly didn't know which direction to go. There village was gone, so they had no real home to return too and now that the land belonged to Normans, that danger was at most present.

An hour passed and they finally came to a small stream. Alana couldn't have been more relieved to get a drink and wash some of the grime from her body.

"We'll rest here." She said to Nettie, pushing her sleeves upward as she knelt to palm some water.

Nettie sank against a rock and swept her forearm across her brow. "I'm so hungry, Alana."

"Let's take a minute to rest and than look for food." Just as she said that, a sudden rustling came from the opposite side of the stream.

Her heart lurched against her chest as she sprang to her feet, her eyes widening as three men on horseback broke through the clearing.

"Alana-" Nettie's voice, threaded with fear, came from behind as all three pairs of eyes settled on them.

Fallon woke to the blinding afternoon light and an insistent ache in his head with no memory to the previous night's events.

Groaning, he rolled away from the window and let his feet fall to the floor. He dropped his head in his palms and waited for the room to cease spinning wildly out of place.

Raising his head, he waited for his vision to clear before making an attempt to stand on two feet. How much mead did he consume to get so sloshed?

Cursing his feeble mastery when it came to honeyed liquor, he vowed to not touch the wretched drink again as he clumsily slipped into a tunic.

Sweeping a hand through his tangled mane, he started for the door and found a sleeping Ivan by his door.

"Ivan!" he growled, and realized his mistake as the ache in his head grew to a fierce throbbing.

Ivan hastened to his feet and struggled to conceal his knowing smirk.

Catching a hint of his man's grin, Fallon said through clenched teeth, "I am in a foul mood to hear any of your jesting, so refrain from your quips and tell me why you are sitting at my door?"

"You asked me too." Ivan replied his voice laced with that casual sarcasm.

Fallon raised a golden brow, "What?"

Ivan struggled to keep from laughing, "It seems that your betrothed is quite taken with you and last night after a few, well many pitchers of mead, you were quite besotted with your wife-to-be." He fell silent, letting Fallon's muddled mind absorb the words, "-well you wooing the lass-"

"Enough!" Fallon shouted, throwing up his hand, not wanting to hear anymore. Clearly he was far too drunk last night to even tell the difference from his bride-to-be to the woman that plagued his groin.

"Milord!" shouted Gavin as he came around the corner to where he and Ivan stood.

He resisted another groan as he cast a dark glare on the man. "What is it?" he snapped.

"The servant, Nettie, she has gone missing."

Suddenly, the fogginess in his head began to clear. He straightened, realizing he had not seen Alana at all the previous day. "The woman was not in the hall last night?"

Both Ivan and Gavin shared a glance, "Nay, milord."

Mumbling a stream of curses under his breath, Fallon shoved the two men aside and stalked down the hall. With each step, his anger intensified along with a slight inkling of dread.

This time, he did not knock, but instead, broke through the door to find her room empty and her bed untouched.

"Dammit!" he spun around and met his men in the hall. "Saddle the horses!"

Alana felt her blood run cold as alarm crept through her limbs as one by one, all three men dismounted, each casting the other a sideways glance and curved sneers, turning her fear to dread.

"You bonny chits lost?" the man in the middle was the first to speak. He was the tallest of the three and perhaps the most disturbing to look at.

His face was matted with a few days growth of beard, lips that were cracked peeled back from a set of crooked teeth with a daunting, black stare that swept the length of her, churning her stomach.

The two men on the outer side inched their way further apart from the man in the middle, slowly making their way through the stream.

Alana took a step back, "We're not lost." She had wanted to sound assertive and certain but her shrilly voice betrayed her fear.

From behind, she felt Nettie pressed against her, trembling uncontrollably. As the men grew closer, she began inching further back.

"Could we be of some aid?" his throatiness tone made her tremble inwardly; his shrewd eyes settled fervently on her breasts and she felt her heart leap in her throat.

As the men closed in on them, she realized than how terrified Nettie must have felt that day in the village and suddenly felt very frightened and vulnerable.

She spun around and shoved Nettie, "Run!"

The fear and adrenaline combined willed her flight. The sound of the men crashing through the shrubbery was like a violent thrashing in her ears along with a fierce pulse, realizing the latter was her heart, threatening to burst from her chest.

She pushed Nettie before her and ushered her to continue as she made an attempt to thwart their pursuers, grabbing whatever she could find to use as an obstruction, not realizing, she put further distance between her and Nettie, until suddenly, she was very alone.

A lump of fear lodged tightly in her throat as she swept the area for her cousin but could see only trees. The sound of earth being trampled forced her to a standstill. As the sound grew deafening she spotted a large rock and swept it into her palm.

She started running in the direction she last saw Nettie but as she did, a man leapt from the hill and landed right in her path.

Forcing the scream back down her throat, she gritted her teeth and sprang back. As the man stood, she hid the rock in a fold of her skirt and took another step away from him.

"Don't come any closer." The voice that rose from her throat was hollow and weak, so unlike her, that it nearly swayed her to tears.

"You frightened of us, lass?" Alana spun around, startled to see the bearded man coming down the trail.

Her stomach coiled with panic, realizing she was trapped. She stood still as the man approached her, his dark eyes moving hungrily over her as he grew closer.

When he stood directly over her, she remained frozen as he reached out and captured a red strand. "Pretty."

The sight of her hair clutched in his grimy, twig-like fingers, was so disturbing opposed to the memory of Fallon's large, callused hand that she jerked back and the strand fell free.

The man's black eyes danced wickedly over her face as he chuckled under his breath, sparring his friend a glance. "You going to fight me, lass?"

She took a fleeting breath before his arm lashed out and jerked her against him. Frightened by the strength in his grip, she shoved against his chest as laughter rumbled from his throat.

"Come now, I'm not going to hurt you." He reached up and gripped her chin cruelly between his fingers and captured her mouth roughly.

Adjusting her grip around the rock, she brought her arm upward with as much force and planted it firmly against his temple.

The instant his arms fell away, she made a dash for freedom but cried out as a set of male arms enclosed around her, dragging her backward.

As the other man lifted her squirming limbs into his arms, he laughed eagerly, carrying her with ease to the bearded man.

"She's a hellion!" her captor teased before setting her down to seize her flailing arms.

The bearded man came to stand over her and her eyes settled on the blood oozing from a gash in his forehead. The anger that sparked in his eyes was enough to make the blood flee her face but she resisted showing fear and instead raised her head to match his glare.

"You'll pay dearly for that one, wench."

Chapter 26

Her captor loomed above her, blood seeping from a nasty split in his temple and all the anger glinting from his eyes as he reached down and pulled a dirk from his waist-belt.

Alana grew breathless and lightheaded as he raised the blade, leveling the tip with her eyes.

"What do you think, Ives, a scar for a scar?"

The man called Ives tightened his grip around her wrists as he pinned them to her back, holding her firmly in place as the bearded man wielded the small blade before her face.

Riveted with fear, Alana had not noticed a shadow garbed all in black, standing beyond her captor's shoulder.

The moment her eyes averted from her captor's, he whirled around, surprised to find a stranger observing them through piercing, silver eyes.

Alana's heart did a strange flip in her chest the moment she recognized the stranger. She had not realized how terrified she had been of her captors until relief at seeing Curran, flooded through her.

"Something interests you, stranger?" her captor grumbled, leisurely waving his blade in the air as if unmoved by the sudden interruption.

Alana watched Curran's face, noting the grim set of his mouth, the keen sharpness to his icy stare as he regarded the two men with due deliberation. She had recognized that hardness before, that cutting gleam that eventually led to bloodshed.

His mouth twisted into a sudden grin as he stepped toward them, the sun glinting off his black breeches as he motioned to the woman trapped between them. "I was merely wondering if you'd be willing to share her."

Alana's heart dropped and all relief turned to disbelief.

Her captor snickered as he turned back around to her. "I don't think you could handle her, mister."

"On the contrary-" Curran's voice grew closer and her captor's face creased with growing irritation. There was a sudden whoosh in the air and Alana flinched as her captor went stiff, his eyes growing wide with a dying light as he stumbled away from her, the dirk falling to her feet as he staggered around to face Curran, exposing his punctured back, blood seeping a dark path through his clothing.

Curran shuffled his sword from one hand to the other, catching the hilt with relaxedness as he stepped toward Ives. "Do you share your dead-friend's word?"

Alana gritted her teeth as his fingers tightened painfully around her wrists, "We can share her, stranger."

Curran shook his dark head, "I don't share." He raised his blade, coated in the bearded man's blood, and wielded it. Ives shoved her aside, brandishing his sword and the air was severed with steel.

The sudden momentum set her off balance and she hit the ground with a painful thud. She rolled to her feet and moved to put distance between them, all the while, watching as Curran entangled his blade, meeting each blow with precision and exactness. Alana knew the other man was no match for Curran's adeptness and skill but her attacker continued, growing weaker under Curran's advances.

The moment Ives hit the ground, Alana turned away, knowing Curran would show no mercy. She heard a distinct grunt as steel cut through flesh and she cringed inwardly.

When she felt it was safe to raise her head, she was surprised to find Curran kneeling by his opponent, rummaging through his pockets.

"You're going to steal from him?" she asked, slightly perturbed.

Curran stood and pocketed his findings and than turned and fixed her with a hard stare. "He just tried to ravish you and you're concerned about me stealing from him?"

Alana's eyes widened remembering a third man. "There was another man." And than remembering Nettie, her heart lurched with dread. "Nettie!"

As she swept by Curran, she was startled when his hand reached out and grasped her arm. "What are you doing?" she said alarmingly.

"We're leaving."

Her blood turned cold, "I'm not leaving my cousin."

His silver eyes hardened as he tugged her toward him, "I didn't come for her."

Rosalind awoke later feeling hopeful and quite pleased with herself. Last night couldn't have gone more according to plan; it had all fallen directly where she expected, without that red-haired servant around to distract Fallon, she now can work her irresistible charm.

She grinned inwardly as she dressed, remembering the prior evening and how Fallon had practically fallen into her lap. She had not been pleased by the amount of drink he had tossed but that would soon change once she was mistress of Linden.

She was far more beautiful than that ninny of a serf; surely he would see that now that she was no longer around to flaunt her strange colored hair and unusual eyes.

Taking a minute to perfect her hair, she left her room and went in search of her betrothed. She found the hall completely deserted. She grew unnerved to find Fallon's men also absent.

She caught a servant in the hall. "Where is Lord Fallon?" she demanded.

The girl merely peered back at her with surprise, "He has gone, milady."

Rosalind frowned, "Gone?"

"He left an hour ago-"

"Do you know where he went?"

The girl shook her head, "Nay, milady."

"Ah!" Rosalind cried in dismay, stamping her foot before shooing the girl away.

Gathering her skirts, she stalked the halls, hoping to find a serf who knew her betrothed's whereabouts. This was not what she had anticipated when waking. She knew of only one servant that was the eyes and ears of Linden and when she spied Matilda she motioned the paunchy woman to her.

"Good day, milady." The woman cried cheerfully.

If not for the serf's eagerness to please her, she would be thoroughly disgusted by the butterball and her poor attempts at managing her unwieldy appearance.

She feigned a smile to hide her revulsion, "Matilda, have you inkling as to my betrothed's whereabouts?"

"He and the others left earlier, milady, it would seem that Saxon-" her face turned beet-red remembering that her mistress was Saxon and quickly mend her wording, "-red-haired serf went missing last eve."

Rosalind's temper erupted. "He is chasing after a serf?"

Matilda stepped back, surprised by her sudden outburst, "Aye, milady." And than quickly she added, "Master Fallon will see to punishing that girl for running, you will see."

On that note, Rosalind's nostrils flared wide as she inhaled a deep steady breath at the satisfying illustration. "I hope you're right, Matilda. I for one do not tolerate rebellion."

Matilda thumped away and Rosalind huffed beneath her breath. She made a mental note of getting rid of Matilda once she was mistress of Linden. She didn't need a servant moving about with heavy-footing listening in on her every word.

Chapter 27

Alana's heart lurched against her chest as she stared up at Curran, unsure if she had heard him correctly. "What?"

His fingers tightened around her arm, "You're mine now, Alana. I'm taking you back to Linden with me." He said gruffly, pulling her after him.

She dug her heels into the ground, "I'm not going anywhere with you!"

"You don't have a choice." He growled, turning around and lifting her up over his shoulder.

She cried out in frustration and began pummeling his back, kicking fiercely in an attempt to wiggle free.

He chuckled as he walked with ease to where his horse waited. "Is that how you show your savior any gratitude?"

"Savior?" she mocked, "You are no savior, you blackheart!"

He laughed as he set her down by his horse. He reached out and gripped her chin. "I saved your life, lass, don't you think I deserve an award?"

Her green eyes sparked daggers, "Not ever."

He laughed and she stiffened as he traced a line the length of her cheek. "Your anger only accents your beauty."

Her eyes grew round as he tilted his head, realizing his meaning, she pushed against his chest. He snickered at her meager struggles and gripped her neck, stilling her as his mouth captured her lips roughly. Her struggling intensified beneath the pressure of his mouth. His kiss roughened, bruising, as he forced his tongue entry.

He grasped her waist and jerked her against him. Panic tore through her as she felt his arousal, pressing against her stomach.

She opened her mouth to him and the kiss deepened, as a moan surfaced from his throat, she sank her teeth into his bottom lip.

He reared back, tasted blood and hissed a violent curse.

Trapped between Curran and horse, Alana could do no more than watch the anger contort his dark face.

For a fraction of a second, she was truly terrified, but considering all she had endured, pushed her fear back into a hollow place, and tilted her chin, meeting his enraged stare.

"You may strike me all you wish, but rest assured, I will put up a damn good fight." Nudging her chin a little higher, she persisted, "If you have the intention of ravishing me, than best rely on the notion that I will kill you before I allow you to put your hands on me again."

The only sound to permit the silence was her hammering heart as she watched the emotions shift in his face, and than he surprised her by grinning and he said, "I intend to ravish you after I've married you."

The thoughts that raced through Fallon's mind drew him near to hysteria. He had never encountered such a feeling, not even in the depths of bloodshed and war, had he experienced it.

As his mind conjured horrors that could befall a woman as beautiful as Alana, he felt that pang of certain fear and had a fierce urge to hold her in his arms.

Any feelings he had felt he thought connected to the basis of his hunger for her. He believed once he sedated his lust, she would no longer be of interest to him, but the very thought of harm becoming her, nearly drove him to the edge of madness.

If he found her, unharmed, he would be the one ringing her pretty little neck and than after, he would do what he has wanted to do since the moment he first laid eyes on her.

"Milord!" Ranulf called, drawing him from his thoughts, "There is something up ahead."

Wrapping his fingers tighter around his sword, he followed the direction of Ranulf's hand and was surprised to see a woman coming there way but the woman was not Alana.

Gavin was the first to break forward, urging his horse into a canter.

Seeing Alana's cousin alone caused his heart to turn over in fear. He motioned his horse forward and came to where Gavin had intercepted her.

"Are you alright-"

"Where is Alana?" he demanded, cutting into Gavin's concern.

Startled, and seemingly shaken, she peered up at him with tearful blue eyes. She hugged her trembling body and her shoulders slumped in dismay.

"What happened?" Ivan asked from behind Fallon.

Ranulf was silent, observing the woman with a strange, hard gleam.

Gavin removed his cloak and gently wrapped her in it.

Growing more alarmed by the girl's silence, Fallon pushed by Gavin and seized the girl's arm. "Speak, dammit!"

"Enough!" Gavin stepped between them, unclasping Nettie from Fallon's iron grip. "You're frightening her."

"Step aside, Gavin." Fallon growled through clenched teeth.

"We were attacked." Her voice was barely a whisper, but enough to stay the two men.

"How many?" Fallon demanded.

Her pale face streaked in tears, turned up to him. "There were three."

"What happened?"

"Alana told me to run, so I did-" she broke into a sob, "-she was right behind me."

Gavin stepped forward and pulled her gently into his arms. She turned into his shoulder and wept quietly.

Clenching his jaw as a hard knot formed in his gut, he turned and stalked back to his horse. "Take the girl home." As he picked up his reins, he pointed to Ranulf, "You'll come with me. Ivan will go with Gavin."

"Alana!" Nettie's cry forced Fallon to go still in his saddle, his amber eyes swept around and was startled to see Curran coming up the trial with Alana sitting before him.

Nettie took off at a run and Alana jumped down from the saddle, rushing to intercept her cousin.

He didn't realize he gripped the reins fiercely until a pain rushed up his arm. His eyes met his brother's from across the distance as he dismounted and his jaw hardened.

"Gavin, take the girl back to Linden." He growled darkly.

Gavin nodded and gently pried the two women apart.

"Do you wish for me to stay, my liege?" Ranulf asked his scarred face furrowing with displeasure as his eyes connected with Curran's.

Fallon shook his head as he came to stand at Alana's side. "Nay."

As Ivan and Gavin swung there horses around, with Nettie sitting before Gavin, Ranulf hesitated, noting the ominous look in Fallon's eye but did as his Lord bid.

Once the three of them were alone, Fallon was the first to speak, "Thank you, brother, for returning my slave." As he said this lastly, he turned to Alana.

She winced beneath the remark.

Curran, still sitting atop his horse, leaned forward and placed his hands on the pommel. "I merely saved my bride."

Alana felt Fallon's body stiffen by her side as all the fury permeated from his amber eyes.

Curran's silver eyes danced sideways to where Alana stood, "She's a beautiful woman, brother."

"Where do you come off stealing my slaves?" Fallon snapped the muscle at his jaw tensing.

A dark brow rose as Curran straightened in his saddle, "Stealing?" he laughed, "You seem to forget she ran, which means she's up for the taking."

He turned and cast Alana with a hard glare. He was beyond angry. He was on the verge of killing them both with his bare hands.

He couldn't read her expression or the emotion in her green eyes but he was far too heated to think of her feelings. Did she think him such a beast to run?

He turned away from her and mounted, all the while, feeling her green eyes boring into his back. He caught up his reins and turned to address Curran. "Let's see if you can tame her as I've been unable to do." He avoided her stare and kicked his horse into a run.

Chapter 28

He could kill. So enraged by his brother's actions and Alana's compelling urge to escape him, she now unwittingly put herself up for grabs. He could throttle her!

The fact that his betrothed remained at Linden did little to appease his anger. Inhaling deeply through his nose, he paused to brace his hands on the table, every muscle in his being taut with unimaginable rage.

Damn Curran to hell!

Well, if she thought him such a damned beast she would find out just exactly the type of beast he could be.

He had prolonged the inevitable. He had a duty to his King, and though he greatly disapproved of it, William wished to greater his alliances, forcing him to wed.

He had sought after Alana's skirts like a youthful lad wet behind the ears. She had made her second mistake by running, her first, saving a man that most wished dead.

Of all men expected to take a wife, he never thought Curran the sort.

He swept his arm across the table, sending an empty tankard soaring across the room.

So in wrapped in his thoughts, he had not seen the woman entering the hall.

"Milord?"

He straightened from the table and swept a hand through his tousled hair. "What can I do for you, milady?" he struggled to conceal the ire in his tone as he turned to his betrothed.

Rosalind bit down on her own anger, sensing his, she knew now was not a good time to tell him how she felt about her betrothed chasing a serf all over Canterbury.

"Is there aught I can do for you?" she had taken extra care in her appearance, ensuring to look her best for him now that the red-haired serf was no longer a hindrance.

Her hair, usually pulled into a chignon, now splayed her shoulders in an inky blanket of curls. Her face flushed crimson did wonders for her dark eyes and her lips, a rosy-pink, usually inspired flavorful glances, but as she stood before her betrothed, she sensed all her efforts went unnoticed.

She lowered her sooty lashes as she felt his eyes upon her, "I wish to please you, milord."

Fallon took a moment to study his bride. Their first encounter, he remembered her as shy and slightly wary of him.

He stepped from around the table and approached her, he watched her carefully, taking note of the tensing of her shoulders. "Do you fear me, bride?"

The question startled as well as unnerved her. She peered up from beneath her lashes to look at him. "Yes, milord."

Her fear of him magnified his ire. He sensed her eagerness to become Mistress of Linden but with that, came a price. He sensed no real spark of attraction in this woman, with Alana, there was fire and passion and he couldn't simply let another man, even if that man were his brother, take her.

Whether she refused to admit that she felt the same way, he would prove to her that those feelings are very real and fated.

"You will sup with me tonight?"

She seemed slightly surprised by his request, but she nodded, "Aye, milord."

As Rosalind slipped from the hall, she felt all the excitement in her, brimming to the surface. Her plan had worked! He was showing interest, soon, he would be eating from the palm of her hand.

Her excitement died at the sight that greeted her in the corridor. The man, who had arranged all her plans in seeing the red-haired serf gone, was coming toward her, dragging the object of all her hatred, in tow.

Her face flushed a deep red as she stalked toward him, her fists clenched at her sides as she stepped in his path. "What is this?" she demanded, wagging a finger at Alana. "You said she would be gone!" she hissed, "What is she doing here?"

Curran's face darkened with menace, "I said you would get what you want, and so you did."

"That was not our agreement!" Rosalind snapped, eying Alana with coldness.

Curran stepped toward her and she stiffened, "Than you misunderstood me."

He brushed past her and pulled Alana after him, leaving Rosalind glowering after them.

"You arranged my escape?" Alana asked as she wrenched away from him.

Curran grinned as he closed his chamber door and turned to peer at her. "So I did."

Her chest rose and fell with sudden outrage, "You nearly got us killed!"

"Aye, and I saved you, so that makes us square." He stepped toward her and raked her from head to toe.

Alana's heart jumped warily against her breast as she stepped around him. "I'd rather die than let you touch me."

His mouth curved into a wry grin as he mirrored her steps, "Fear is most unfitting on you."

"Pig." She hissed.

He laughed, "That is more like it."

She moved to put a table between them, "I won't marry you."

He tilted his head at her, "There is no one to prevent that from happening, it would seem my brother does not want you anymore."

She had not dwelled on how Fallon had coldly turned his back on her and how strangely painful that blow had dealt her heart, instead, she ignored those thoughts and jerked her chin upward. "Find another."

His laughter snaked down her spine in a cold chill as he advanced towards her; she gave a short cry as she lunged for the door but his arm stopped her flight, reeling her against him. "There is no other with your fiery spirit."

She pushed him away and he released her easily, stepping back and laughing as if her distress amused him. "There is nothing that will change my opinion of you. You attacked my cousin, my village; all those innocent people are dead because of you."

He turned his back to her and poured a glass of mead. "It's nothing personal, just war."

Her eyes narrowed sharply on his back, "It was personal to me."

He turned back around and leaned against the table, drinking heavily of his mead while his eyes danced over the length of her. "I feel nothing for your dead village, so if that fuels your hatred of me, than good, I revel in that."

Alana could have flew at him, scratched all the cold amusement from his wicked face, but she knew he was taunting her, encouraging her to fight him, and she wouldn't give him the pleasure.

Instead, she straightened and moved to the door. He made no move to stop her and for that, she was grateful, because as she stepped into the hall, she erupted into tears.

Chapter 29

The evening meal came all too quickly. Alana found herself seated at the very table with the object of her brooding thoughts sitting to the left of her.

She felt many eyes upon her and focused intently on her untouched plate to avoid them.

A woman cleared her throat, that woman; sitting across from her, was Rosalind.

"Forgive my obtuseness, but I thought serfs ate with the rest of the lowly peasants, not at the table with their Lord?"

Alana lifted her head and her eyes connected sharply with Rosalind's sullen black stare and she felt a redness creep in her cheeks as all eyes turned on her.

The man to Alana's right shifted in his chair and corrected sternly, "She is my betrothed-" Curran was quick to reply, "It would be uncomely to have my soon-to-be-wife sitting elsewhere."

Rosalind shied away from Curran's heavy stare and clamped her mouth shut, silently seething.

Alana glanced from beneath her lashes to sneak a chance at Fallon. He had been silent all throughout dinner and appeared very much displeased in having her present.

She would have done anything to avoid this happening but Curran had not given her much of a choice.

His food remained untouched, all but his mead, which he gripped menacingly in one hand. His face was taut and expressionless.

Her heart ached at the sight of him.

How did she come into this mess?

She would have done anything to avoid marrying Curran.

Fallon was suddenly on his feet and exiting the hall. Alana watched him go, surprised at how calm and quietly he had left the table.

She would have done anything to know his thoughts.

Another chair scraped against the stone floor. Alana turned and caught eyes with Rosalind. Turning her nose upward in a haughty manner, Rosalind gathered her skirts and followed Fallon's departure.

The meal carried on and Alana waited until she felt it a good time to retire. Curran entertained his meal and the company of his men, paying little heed to her as she arose from the table and quietly left the hall.

She was tired she realized, slipping into the darkened corridor, so tired, that she hadn't noticed the massive shadow leaning casually against the stone wall, watching her intently.

"Alana."

She froze, startled as Fallon stepped toward her. "Fallon?" she frowned, "What do you do?"

His gold eyes leveled on her face, "Does it please you?"

Her brows knitted together at the question, "Does what please me, Fallon?"

His beautifully handsome face grew taut, "To become my brother's wife?"

She was startled by the question, even more so by the scowl that darkened his face, "He saved my life."

His jaw clenched, "So naturally, you would consent to marry him?"

She tilted her chin, "I have no intention of marrying anyone, nor do I intend to have this conversation, you're head is clearly clouded."

He stepped in her path, hindering her escape, "I won't let you marry my brother."

Her green eyes narrowed deliberately, "Good."

"You will marry me." He growled,

Alana felt the floor tilt beneath her feet at his declaration. Her heart did a strange flutter as well as her stomach. She peered at him as if he had lost his marbles, yet, within, a part of her had waited to hear him say those words, confess some semblance of what she thought had been a blossoming love between them. Did this mean he loved her? Or could he not abide the thought of another man having her because he had yet to stake his claim on her virtue?

She shut down any hopeful feelings and instead, hardened her heart. "Do you forget? You are already betrothed. Your King would not be thrilled if you violated your oath. You see what becomes the enemy when they betray your king? Must you tempt that path?"

He inhaled deeply through his nose, and his large chest broadened with it. "I do not desire Rosalind as I desire you."

Despite her best efforts to reveal little of her feelings, she felt compelled to say the words that arose in her throat. "So naturally, you would wed me, just to bed me?"

Say it. She demanded silently. Tell me that you love me and I will give myself to you freely. She was surprised that the thought came so naturally, so eagerly to her, and the truth behind it, was even more startling.

His gold eyes burned precariously in the dark, "Curran does not deserve you."

"And you do?"

He grinned, "You were made for me, Alana. I've held you in my arms; your body fits perfectly to mine."

She shook her head, "That doesn't mean anything."

He stepped toward her and she felt her insides stir, "You know that it does." He reached out and cupped her cheek. "I have wanted you the moment I laid eyes on you. You revived me with your kindred heart. Your gentle touch awakens a fire in me. It means more than a mere tumble." His eyes settled on her mouth, "I will have you as my wife-" he fell silent, teasing her jaw with feather-like caresses, "-even if I must defy my king, and betray my brother."

Chapter 30

The next day, Alana could think of none other than the words Fallon had whispered earnestly to her in the hall.

Even now, as she recalled his troth, she felt a sliver of fear. She could not allow him to betray William, or Curran, no matter how great her revulsion for the man, she didn't have the heart to sever those bonds and potentially hurt him in some way.

To his king, Fallon was a liability, as well as to his people, though they denied him, she saw Fallon for the equal and fair man that he was.

"I ponder, whose face you envision, to bring such a look to your eyes."

Alana spun around, so absorbed in her thoughts; she hadn't heard her chamber door open.

Her eyes narrowed angrily on Curran, relaxed against the wall, "You do not have the liberty to come and go as you please among my chambers." She raised her chin, "Get out."

The uncanny glint that magnified the gray of his eyes altered to that piercing silver as he pushed away from the wall, stepping toward her.

Once again, she was given the impression of a wolf, and oh, how she longed for her lion.

"You are my betrothed..." his voice held a tinge of anger, a slight mixture of determination- "If it suits me to have you in my sight at all hours of the day, than I shall do so, perhaps I may even use a manacle to link you permanently to my ankle?"

Her chest rose with a violent breath. He was taunting her; pulling on her defiant strings to trigger a response. She knew he reveled in that; her defiance, her fiery nature.

He came to stand over her, his silver eyes hardening with disappointment, "You have naught to say from that pretty mouth?" his expression darkened, "Your heart belongs to my brother, but I will see to breaking that."

Rosalind flattened her body against the wall as Curran stepped into the hall; her mouth thinning into a grim line.

This just wouldn't do. She and Curran had an agreement, unfortunately for her; he failed to mention his own motives of their arrangement.

She wanted Alana gone! Far from Fallon's sight and touch. The very thought of her husband-to-be touching another woman left her livid.

She would not abide it. They were to marry and she intended to have her fearsome husband all to herself. She certainly wasn't willing to share him, especially with a lowly serf. What could he possibly see in that insufferable peasant? Her hair was too red, to rich of a color to catch any man's wandering eye. Her eyes were unusual, too extraordinary.

Rosalind grimaced. No, this just would not do.

She would have to see in ridding herself of the wretched girl and who best to do the task but herself?

Fallon had searched the hall all midday for Alana, but she hadn't turned up anywhere. It disturbed him deeply to know that Curran could be following her shadow. His brother was not to be trusted, especially with a woman as beautiful as Alana.

Yet, he was not a fool to the emotions reflected there in those damning silver eyes. Curran would never admit it, but Fallon believed him capable of loving Alana.

Curran had never loved, of that, he was certain. His brother was a man driven only by influential power and the obsession to be unconquerable.

Curran was exceptionally skillful as a warrior; swift and agile on foot, undeniably lethal with hilt in hand, but his insatiable thirst to be unrivaled could potentially be his downfall. He was at times brash and impulsive, and that led to mistakes, and mistakes lead to death.

Once again, Curran had faulted, that mistake being Alana.

Brother or not, ally or adversary, Fallon would not be swayed in his decision to have Alana. She belonged to him and no other. She was his woman and he would see to staking claim on what was rightfully his.

He made his way to the hall and nearly collided with one of the serfs. "My apologies, milord." The man produced a missive, "This just arrived for you."

He accepted the missive and ripped open the seal while Ranulf made his way down the corridor towards him. "What is it, my liege?"

"It's William-" Fallon muttered, his eyes roaming the script, "He's coming to Linden."

Chapter 31

Word of William's arrival spread vastly through Linden, triggering an immediate response in all the serfs to work diligently in preparation for the King.

Rosalind was thoroughly petrified.

She had heard much gruesome talk of William from his fierce countenance to his unmerciful manner.

She was quite sure that William would show her very little courtesy and lenience. She was after all the daughter of a Saxon trying to keep his lands on Norman territory.

Did William come to Linden to access their agreement?

She would be happy to tell the King that her supposed husband-to-be wanted absolutely nothing to do with her but everything to do with a simple-minded serf!

Mayhap having William come to Linden could work to her advantage?

Her father was a tenacious man; she had never seen the look of fear in his eyes, until now. He was in fear of losing his lands and it was up to her to ensure that doesn't happen.

She couldn't allow Fallon's infatuation with a serf to corrupt that.

William had agreed to their bargain, surely he would disapprove of a serf getting in the way of that? Mayhap if she explained he would simply do away with Alana.

She was so enlightened by the thought; she gathered her skirts and went in search of her husband-to-be. She had every means of revealing her intentions to Fallon for he would know that nothing would stand in the way of their arrangement.

When she found him, he was training in the field, bathed in perspiration, muscle gleaming beneath the sun; a magnificent work of man-all women would envy her.

"My lord, I would have a word with you." She called, drawing his golden glare.

He appeared annoyed with her demand but simply handed his sword to a man standing nearby and walked toward her. "What have you, milady?"

"I intend to speak with the King when he arrives."

She had hoped to spark some sort of response in him but his face remained expressionless and so she continued, hoping to rile him. "My father and your King made an arrangement and I have attempted on my part, you however, fail to acknowledge any of it and instead chase after the skirts of another-shall I bring this to your Lordship's attention?"

She caught the flicker of anger, the sudden rush of temper for his eyes flared brighter, more pronounced in their brilliant amber as he said very sternly. "Lady Rosalind-" his voice was flat, lacking any warmth on her part. "-I have every intention of addressing my King on the matter, however, for a reason entirely of my own." He stepped toward her and she had to swallow, suddenly robbed of her breath of his nearness. "You see-" he said very carefully, "-I have no intention of marrying you and I will find every means possible of escaping this damned agreement."

Her mouth fell open as he turned and stalked away, leaving her to glare outraged at his back.

How dare him! Dismiss her so easily?

Her nails dug into her palms until they bled. So he thought to rid him of her that quickly? She was a McLeod!

Spinning angrily around on her heels, she stalked towards the keep. She'd be damned if she was going to allow this to happen.

William arrived as accordingly, bringing with him significant artillery to be reckoned with. This somewhat unnerved Fallon though it was not uncommon for a King to travel so heavily, it bothered Fallon that his King thought himself threatened while at Linden.

"Linden is indeed a spectacular stronghold; you have done well in managing it." William said appreciatively as they entered the great hall.

A serf moved forward to offer a silver tray of ale as they settled at the trestle table, William's dark, intense stare moving about the room.

"Will you be staying unto the evening, my liege?"

William dismissed the servant and reached for his canter. "Perhaps I shall, for I find myself certainly famished, if you intend to feed your King?" he smirked over the rim of his goblet.

Fallon grinned, "I shall indeed; a feast is being prepared as we speak."

"Good, good." William chimed, setting his canter aside. "And how does your betrothed fare?"

Fallon cringed inwardly. He had been dreading this conversation since word of William's arrival and hadn't anticipated speaking of it already.

Thankfully, he hadn't a chance to respond for a serf appeared to announce that supper would be done shortly.

He quickly sought a change of topic. "How goes the construction in Lincoln?"

A look of pride glinted sharply in William's dark eyes. "Lincoln is flourishing." William's dark eyes peered at Fallon knowingly. "You avoid speaking of your betrothed-why is that?"

Fallon shifted uncomfortably in his seat a feeling he found completely disconcerting for it was difficult to make 'The Fury' uncomfortable.

"Are you displeased with the McLeod woman?"

Fallon met that unyielding stare. "Nay."

A heavy, dark brow lifted. "Is she uncomely than?"

"Nay-" he spoke truthfully, Rosalind was beautiful but a vision of someone more lovely rushed to mind. "-I find our arrangement disagreeable." He knew he was teetering on dangerous grounds, but he would have his King know that he had no intention of marrying Rosalind. "We are simply not suited."

A muscle twitched along William's jaw. "I care not if you are suited-we agreed upon this arrangement to ensure McLeod's allegiance-do you now renege our bargain?"

"You know where my loyalty stands but I shan't marry the woman."

He could detect that calculating coldness behind that sharp glare. He was risking much, going against his King but he knew, without doubt, he would risk anything to have Alana.

As if sensing his thoughts, William suddenly peered at him anew. "Something has changed in you, Fury."

Fallon arched a golden brow, "My liege?"

William tilted his head, studying Fallon with certain aware-ness. "Aye, something indeed."

Once again, he felt uncomfortable and shifted uneasily.

"Perhaps a woman-not the McLeod, for it would seem you are clearly against marrying her, if not she, than whom?" William's sudden interest in Alana did not sit well with him.

"She is of no significance." He tried deterring William's in-terest.

"She must be something to ensnare the heart of 'The Fury'."

He remained silent.

"This woman, is she here?"

He bit down on a response, refusing to reveal too much. If William saw fit, he could easily take Alana from him simply because she was Saxon, simply because she had unusual eyes, no matter the reason, if William decreed it, there wasn't much he could do to stop him.

He nodded grudgingly.

"Will she be dining with us?"

His stomach rolled for he was certain it wasn't a question though it was said in that manner. William expected Alana to be there.

"Aye, my liege."

William clasped his hands together, "Good, good. I shall take a gander at this beauty that has captured the heart of the infamous 'Fury'; mayhap I may even find her to my liking? What say you to that, Fury?"

Fallon curled a fist beneath the table. His first instinct was to lunge across the table at his King and he quickly dismissed the thought. He couldn't expose his feelings for Alana to William for surely it could be used against him, for he had, in some way or another, betrayed his King and it would seem William found a means to parade his anger- Alana.

Chapter 32

"What?" Alana said in a shrilly, panicked voice. "The King has asked for my presence at supper?"

Nettie paled considerably to her right.

Matilda merely presented a staunch expression. "It would appear so, girl. Make yourself look presentable. You shan't disappoint the King."

Alana swallowed back a tight knot in her throat. "I cannot-"

"You don't have a choice." Matilda snapped, "The King has asked specifically for you-if you refuse to show, surely you'll face dire consequences." With that, the ample woman strolled from the room.

"What am I to do, Nettie?"

Some color returned to Nettie's face and her cousin turned to fully face her. "You'll go to dinner as requested."

Someone suddenly stormed into the room, startling both her and Nettie. Alana took a step back, somewhat frightened by the sheer anger contorting Curran's face.

"Leave." He growled to Nettie.

Her cousin hastened from the room but not before ex-changing a worried look with Alana and she knew her cousin wouldn't be far from the hall.

"The King suddenly has an interest in you, why is that?" he demanded, stepping toward her.

"I know naught."

"Surely you know–"

"How should I know?" she snapped, "If I did, I certainly wouldn't tell you."

His hand lashed out and he jerked her against him. "I should take you here and now and be done with it!"

Alana felt a tremor run through her but she was deter-mined not to show it. She had heard many a frightening things of Curran and though the thought deeply frightened her, she didn't understand why Curran hesitated to act on his impulses.

She was beginning to wonder if Fallon had been right about Curran. Did Curran truly have strong feelings for her?

His silver eyes fell to her lips and she stiffened. If that were so, her feelings were not the same and she would fight Curran all the way.

Slowly, he unfurled his hand from around her arm. "Dinner will prove to be interesting."

Alana dreaded supper. She hadn't seen Fallon since that previous day and in that moment, she wished she had. Had Fallon said something to provoke the King? Why was he suddenly so interested in her? Was it simply because she was Saxon? Did he view her as a hindrance to Rosalind and Fallon's supposed troth?

She had heard that the Conqueror was a man of ruthless traits. She much doubted he would show her any consideration; he would mostly likely banish her from Linden than crack a smile.

She prolonged and dallied as much as she could but it wasn't long before a subtle knock sounded at her door, proclaiming dinner.

Sighing heavily, she moved to open it and was seemingly startled to find a bristling Rosalind on the other side.

Dark, sloe eyes narrowed angrily. "What have you said to the King?" she demanded.

Alana blanched, "I have said nothing."

"Nonsense!" the woman shrieked in a harsh whisper, "You and Fallon have conspired against me-you have bewitched him! Come, I will have it, what did you say to him?"

Alana raised her chin to level her with an impassive glare. "Whether I spoke with the King or not, I most certainly do not have to tell you."

Rosalind's eyes glinted daggers, "Why you impertinent wench! I could have you flogged you know?"

Alana met her fierce-some glare. "You can try."

A sudden glimmer of something evil brightened her ebony stare. "No need-" Rosalind pursed her lips with a hint of a grin, "-once the King is through with you, I'll have Fallon all to myself."

Alana stiffened and felt a fleeting alarm.

Rosalind smirked as if she had already entangled Fallon and disappeared down the hall, leaving Alana dreading the evening all the more.

Fallon shifted uneasily in his chair, though he attempted to conceal his worries from his King, it proved more difficult as his eyes continuously drew to the doors.

It wouldn't be long before Alana strolled through them, drawing every attention in the room, especially the shrewd, dark leer of William.

He couldn't fathom William's motives. He didn't know whether the King himself intended to take Alana from him, to simply take the problem from the equation, so to speak.

Had Rosalind voiced her opinions?

Even as his eyes scanned the hall, he couldn't find his betrothed and he wondered suspiciously at her whereabouts. Rosalind was not to be trusted, especially when it concerned Alana. She viewed Alana as a threat and he believed Rosalind capable of troubling straits.

"What have you enamored?" William's heavy lilt drew him from his thoughts.

Fallon peered at his King, uncertain if he had heard correctly. "My liege?"

The room grew boisterous as hungry men settled at the table. Fallon's men settled alongside him, while Curran's men settled along the opposite. Fallon took keen notice to Curran's absence.

He drew his attention to his King, "I am not certain I understand you."

The two of them spoke quietly, only loud enough for their ears alone. "I wish to know what has you so enamored of this woman-aside from her beauty."

Fallon resisted a grin, "What makes you think she is beautiful?"

William smirked, "I know you well enough to know that any woman you take to bed is of some exquisiteness."

When Fallon remained silent, William arched a brow at this. "You have yet to bed her?"

Were his thoughts that transparent?

"I do not wish to simply bed her." Had he truly spoken the words aloud?

His response seemed to surprise his King. "I had never thought you capable of love, Fury. Pray tell, how did you come by this woman?"

Fallon bit down on his response. He was slightly taken aback that he and his King were speaking so casually of love but surprisingly it came naturally without hesitation. "She is Saxon."

William's countenance darkened considerably, "I find it a bit disconcerting to think you have fallen for a Saxon maid."

"She saved my life."

William's expression shifted to sheer surprise. "How so?"

"The battle of Hastings-I was attacked and left for dead. She found me, restored me and in return, we attacked her village, killed her people." He felt a swift pang of turmoil seize him, realizing for the first time how terribly painful that must have been for Alana. "Despite being her enemy, she risked much and healed my wounds."

William listened intently but something out of his peripheral drew his attention-he averted his eyes and was caught unexpectedly by a rush of intrigue as a woman with an incredible shade of red hair whisked into the hall.

He grinned with aroused curiosity as the woman made her way to them. "Beautiful indeed, Fury."

Chapter 33

Alana's knees threatened to buckle as she nervously made her way towards where Fallon and the ominous frame of William sat at the head of the long, trestle table.

When the King's dark, brooding stare turned her way, her stomach turned in fear.

Her eyes shifted warily to Fallon whose face remained inexpressive.

She came to where they sat and curtsied, dipping her head in an attempt to avoid the intense, dark eyes regarding her coolly. "My liege." She said softly.

"Stand." The King's strong, commanding voice brought her to her feet.

"Join us." he motioned to an empty seat.

Hesitating, her eyes wavered to Fallon before settling down.

She shifted uneasily as the King studied her with profound interest. "You are quite right, Fallon-" William said, "-she is a beauty."

She glanced from beneath her lashes at Fallon, he sat rigid, the muscles of his face drawn tight and his mouth pulled into a grim line, clearly unnerved by the King's intrigue of her.

William shifted, leaning casually back into his seat, a gesture she hadn't expected from the King, "Tell me-" William started, "-what do you think of your Norman King, my Saxon beauty?"

Did she detect sudden stiffening in Fallon?

Remembering her village destroyed and the innocent massacred, Alana straightened, raised her chin and met the dark gleam that turned in surprise at her unmasked defiance, "I have no real opinion of you milord, merely assumptions."

A dark brow rose curiously, "Pray tell, what are your assumptions, milady?"   She could see a warning glint in Fallon's eye, but Alana was undaunted. This man was responsible for the deaths of innocent people. "You seized our lands with brutality; you killed those innocent of inhabiting it-I find my opinion of you quite bleak."   She could almost feel Fallon's anger from across the table-or was it William's? She wasn't sure.

Silence stretched a fragment but Alana remained firm, refusing to squirm beneath William's piercing glare. She would not be deterred in anger; she thought of those fallen-Rowan, the village men who had defended their families-all the innocent who done naught to deserve such a fate.

And than, the King did the most unexpected thing, surprising not only Fallon, but those in listening range-he laughed!

He tossed back his dark head and chuckled deeply, slamming a hand to the table and rattling a canter.

"I dare say, Fallon, she is by far the most enchanting creature I've encountered-no wonder you've taken an interest in her." Dark, humored eyes slid her way. "What is your name, girl?"

Alana was truly confounded- he found her enchanting, a Saxon? She hadn't expected such a reaction from the infamous, dreaded William the Conqueror.

She lifted her chin, "Alana McKenna."

William's dark eyes glimmered with intrigue. "McKenna? I have heard that name 'afore."

Alana stiffened and particularly noticed a frown creasing Fallon's brow.

"Ah, McKenna-" William started, recognition forming, "-I had heard of a Chieftain McKenna, a man deemed honorable and forthright."

Alana fought a rising of tears as she met William's purposeful stare. "The Chieftain was a fair man-he sought naught but peace among these lands."

William frowned knowingly. "You speak as if you know him personally?"

Alana's shoulders stiffened, "How could I not? The man was my father."

The words spoken from Alana truly startled Fallon. It had never occurred to him to ask about her family-and now that she had revealed a little piece of her, he yearned to know more.

She was the daughter of a Chieftain? It explained so much-her defiance, her determination to protect those innocent-but her fiery nature wasn't entirely due to her upbringing, it was simply who she was.

As William continued to press her with questions, he was keen to note the tensing of her slender shoulders, the glint of unshed tears she struggled to conceal; the pain that clouded her sea-green eyes.

"And what would your father say if he knew you supped with Normans?"

Fallon cursed inwardly for there it was again-pain but she remained collected, carefully regarding William with remoteness. "I imagine my father wouldn't have much to say on the matter-for he is dead."

William straightened at this, thoroughly surprised. "Dead-how so?"

Her lower lip trembled and it went unnoticed beneath William's scrutiny, but not Fallon's.

Raising her chin once more she said, "He was killed, my liege-for defending a hapless village against-" she fell silent.

William arched a brow, "Against?"

She leveled her sea-green eyes defiantly on William. "Normans."

William reached for his canter, but merely wrapped firm fingers around it. "What reason would Normans have for killing your father?"   "What other reasons but for greed?" she said flatly.

"I imagine you feel a certain way about that- your father's death?"

Alana turned her eyes away, peering at her untouched plate. "I would be lying, my liege, if I said I hadn't felt anger towards those who had wronged me-" she lifted her eyes and there a strength glimmered. "-there is no room in my heart for hatred. My father was a courageous man and he died so, protecting a village like the one your men destroyed."

William straightened, "Your father died unjustly for a feeble plight." He said honestly and than added, "As for those who claimed his life, I cannot say who, but not all Normans are accountable for the life of one man."

"I do not fault any Norman." She said truthfully, "My father has taught me to forgive-even those not deserving of it."

"I know this to be fact for you took it upon yourself, despite the dangers to your wellbeing, to rescue a fallen Norman- for that, I am indebted to you." William stated.

Alana's eyes averted fleetingly to Fallon and she quickly drew them away, not wanting to warrant any curious responses from William-but the King was far more aware than she knew.

So absorbed in their conversation, neither three of them had noticed that several men had fallen asleep, others had drifted from the hall, only a few remained and Alana noticed two in particular, careening to the corners-Curran and Rosalind.

"I will grant your appeal, Fallon." William turned in his seat to direct his golden-haired companion, drawing both Alana and Fallon's attention.

What was the King saying?

William's face almost appeared serene at Fallon's awed expression. "My liege?"

Had Alana noticed Curran and Rosalind inching closer as she leaned on the edge of her seat straining to catch each word?

William raised his canter, "You are released of your troth-" his dark eyes slid in Alana's direction. "-you are permitted to marry any woman of your choosing."

Alana's heart did a fierce somersault as her eyes jumped warily to Fallon's jubilant expression.

Two collected gasps of outrage came in union to echo soundly in the hall; in her peripheral, Curran stalked furiously from the hall, leaving an enraged and bemused Rosalind staring confoundedly at the three of them.

Alana quickly escaped the moment she was able, her heart threatening to burst from her chest at any moment.

Had she heard William correctly?

Free of his troth?

Consented to marry any woman of his choosing?

Her heart jumped against her breast at the heated look in Fallon's eyes when he peered at her across the table.

Her skin nearly burned at the image.

What was it that made her stomach flutter madly-the thought of Fallon able to do as he freely pleased, the thought of his claiming her-body and soul?

She was fleeing through the corridors-from Fallon, from her love for him, for the very reasons she imagined not possible were now likely?

She was frightened she concluded as she buried herself within her chamber and pressed her back firmly against the door, taking in a shaky breath.

She could feel so many emotions running through her, she didn't know whether to faint from it or cry out.

She nearly leapt from her skin as a knock sounded at the door.

She backed away from it-uncertain of who waited on the other side-the haughty Rosalind, the furious Curran, the proud King himself, or her golden-haired warrior come to claim his woman?

"Alana?"

Nettie's voice was a sweet beckoned relief.

"What did the King say?" she demanded once inside the chamber.

Alana entangled her hands in her skirts, "He has released Fallon of his betrothal to Rosalind."

Nettie's face revealed open disbelief, "What of Rosalind, and Curran, this will not set well with either one-" and than, she added quickly, "-Curran has already claimed you as his betrothed."

Alana cringed inwardly. She hadn't thought of that since their conversation in the hall. She knew Curran and Rosalind would retaliate in some means-and the thought of Fallon and Curran battling it out, swords in hand, disturbed her greatly. "Can we talk on the morrow?" she asked, feeling a bit nauseated.

Nettie hesitated, as if wanting to say more but thankfully her cousin resisted speaking her fearful notions and quietly left.

Alana moved to settle on the bed and palmed her face; a shudder passing through her.

When another knock sounded at her door, she dropped her hands and stood with a sigh.

"I'm tired, Nettie-" she said, moving to open the door.

She released a sharp breath at the towering, lithe frame standing on the other side. With one effortless push, the door swung open, forcing her to retreat a few paces as Fallon stepped into the room.

He closed the door firmly behind him and raked her from head to toe with open desire.

"What do you want?" she demanded, feeling tingling and warm beneath his heavy, gold stare.

The warm, gentled fire burning low in the hearth caught the vibrant shades of gold in his wild mane. His eyes gleamed intensely as the sharp angles of his face cast shadows from the flickering light.

He stepped toward her; his hands moving to the laces of his tunic, untying them with adapt quickness he tossed the shirt over his head to the floor.

Alana's heart doubled over in fear and exhilaration.

His massive, muscled chest gleamed in the feeble, dancing light as he stepped toward her, "I've come to claim what belongs to me."

Chapter 34

Alana stepped back, driven by fear or the sudden fervor pulsing through her body, she didn't know which.

His nearness alone unraveled her; she felt the proximity of him like a wave of heat, wrapping her in an instant shroud of sensation.

Her eyes of their own accord swept the muscled length of him, the small fire glinting sleekly off his massive chest; her mouth went dry as if he drained her sustenance.

It was so easy to forget he was the infamous warrior known as 'The Fury', though she had witnessed his prowess, his ability to make others fear him, respect him, she could not think of him none other than the gentled-warrior she had rescued from the forest.

She knew that tender side of him others failed to see.

He took a step toward her and she retreated, forcing a frown to his brow. "Do you fear me, Alana?"

She lifted her chin, meeting that amber stare and slowly shook her head.

"Than what is it?"

"I will not have you take me this way." She said purposefully, though within she yearned for his touch, his kiss.

His face furrowed, "Which way?"

Her chin jutted determinedly, "As if I were a piece of property to possess."

She detected a hint of a grin forming at his mouth, "Alana-"

"Nay!" she stayed him with her hand when he took another step. "I mean it, Fallon. Would you have me unwilling?"

He appeared completely taken aback, almost as if he had expected her to come rushing into his open arms-and within, she longed to do so, but she needed to know if his heart ached for her as hers did for him.

She could see the anger forming along with confusion, the uncertainty behind his golden glare, the tension forming in his jaw. "I could have you if it pleases me-"

"Yes, but it would be forced." She held her ground, determined not to be swayed in this. She had endured much emotionally as well as physically-if Fallon wished to claim her, she would see it done properly.

His gold eyes narrowed precariously and she wondered if he would follow through on his threats. "What game is this?" She stiffened, "This isn't a game."

"Than what are you playing at?" he stepped closer and she didn't stop him, "Do you harbor the same feelings as your cousin than?"   Her eyes flashed daggers, "Nettie's fear is justified."

"Than explain it to me." He demanded, moving closer.

Alana inhaled a deep breath through her nose, "Unlike me, Nettie has failed to overcome her demons. Her anger and fear comes from a dark tragedy that lays dormant within her." Her voice faltered as she felt the sting of tears. "Her father was massacred, slain without cause, and her mother brutally attacked-all this done before the eyes of a helpless child."

"This occurred when you were children?" Fallon asked his voice surprisingly soft.

Alana nodded, "This happened the very day my father was taken from me-by Normans." When she lifted her eyes to meet his, a single tear fell free of her lashes.

She tensed when he reached out to gently wipe the wayward tear away. His hand turned and he brushed her cheek with his knuckles. "I am sorry for your loss."

Her heart tugged with the sincerity in his voice, "It is Nettie I fear for. She will never cease to grieve."

"Only time can heal her wounds." Fallon said gently, and than, he trailed his hand to her mouth, tracing her lower lip softly with his thumb. His eyes leveled hotly at that spot, where his thumb gently caressed. "How does one tend to the wounds of a healer?" Her stomach tightened at the gruffness in his voice, the sensual heat flaring in his sun-lit eyes. He pulled her into his arms and she gave little fight. She felt suddenly hapless to his strength. "I am not the same as those who claimed your family-" he said gently, "-of that you know, so what is it that stays you?"

She flattened her hands against the wall of his chest and felt a heat spiral low in her belly at the muscle and warmth there. "I do not wish to be 'claimed'-"

"I will not stand idly aside while others will stop at nothing to have you."   She felt more tears surfacing, tears of anger and frustration.

His arms fell away from her and he stepped back. Immediately she was aware of the draft that settled around her. "William has granted me leave of my betrothal to Rosalind-on that note, I intend to have you as my wife."

Her heart fluttered only than to falter with a disconcerting notion.

She had recalled their conversation in the hall once Curran had announced their troth. Jealousy had prompted Fallon; desire had prompted notions of matrimony. He would simply wed her to ensure that no other could have her, no other, but him.

Her heart yearned for another life entirely-one teeming with love.

She would not marry Fallon simply to sedate his lust, until he understood; she would continue to deny him, though it pained her sorely to do so.

He offered no words of love, instead muttered an oath beneath his breath and swept a callused hand through his mane before stalking from the room.

She flinched when the door slammed closed and she was left staring tearfully where he had disappeared.

The moon sat heavily in the dark-knit sky and all the inhabitants aside from several guards standing post, sipping languidly on mead, slept soundly into the night.

Drifting clouds shifted, baring a stream of moonlight, betraying the hooded-silhouette creeping from the keep.

Claiming a horse, the figure concealed in cloak treaded quietly in the shadows, watching beneath their hood as the guards standing watch drifted into a stupor, their drink forgotten.

Seizing the reins, the body nudged their horse and began a steadfast pace towards the hills. Anger as well as hatred fueled their flight and they rode nonstop into nightfall until reaching the campsite mere miles from Linden.

On arrival, several men gathered to meet the rider, one man in particular separated and moved forward.

"Tomorrow." The rider spieled.

The man nudged his head in acknowledgement and turned to face his men, "We attack at dawn."

Sleep eluded her, as it had done many nights, but this night was far more restless than others, more torturous for her thoughts ceased to settle.

Long after Fallon had left her room, she had laid for some time peering into the darkness of her room. Had she been wrong to turn him away? Was her stubbornness getting in the way of certain hope?

She should have known from the very day she came upon Fallon that she would love him. Mayhap she was being foolish?

She grumbled aloud as she realized once again her thoughts were keeping sleep at bay. She rolled onto her side and clenched her eyes, attempting once more to beckon fatigue.

A slight noise brought her alert and an instant wave of alarm swept through her.

She turned on her back just as a large hand slammed against her mouth, muffling her scream as an arm swept beneath her, wrenching her from her bed.

She buckled and arched against her unseen captor, but the arm latched around her writhing frame only tightened, sucking the air from her lungs.

As she was spun around something distastefully replaced the hand over her mouth, silencing any cries that would have surfaced.

She had little time to react before her wrists were bounded and she was tossed heedlessly over a shoulder and whisked from her room.

Chapter 35

It came as no surprise that Fallon slept little unto the night. His thoughts drifted frequently to Alana, every-nerve ending in his body yearning to go to her.

He had had many a restless nights since bringing Alana to Linden, but this night in particular plagued him more so than others.

She had easily stayed his desires, her heated words preventing him from taking what would have been given easily by countless women, but the very idea of taking her unwillingly churned his gut in the most unsettling way.

A frown creased his brow. He was certain she felt a particular way about him, so why then, did she continuously deny him?

I do not wish to be claimed...

I am not a piece of property to possess...

Aye, it had been that very reason when first he laid eyes upon her; he'd wanted her the way a man desired a woman, but things were different, things had changed. He wanted her for other reasons entirely aside from the basis of lust.

She did inexplicable things to his beating heart. He had never considered the idea of another life, one without war and bloodshed, this life consisting of laughter and love for a woman who would walk alongside him and bare his children.

Did she truly think he would discard her so casually after he's had his fill of her? Surely she knew he had every intention of making her his wife, so why this unwillingness towards him?

He hadn't realized how swiftly night had crept by until the first streaks of early dawn filtered into his chamber.

Certain he would get no sleep; he arose from bed and crossed the room to grab a tunic.

Just as he pulled it on, a resounding knock sounded at his door.

He stiffened; his brows drew together as he started toward it. Who would be at his door at this early hour?

Another knock came, this one a little more persistent than the last and then, a voice- "Milord?"   Fallon frowned, certain he had heard incorrectly. Why would Curran's man be at his door?

Averting his eyes briefly to search the remnants of his room, he found his dirk and sheathed it in the sleeve of his tunic, returned to the door and opened it ajar to peer suspiciously at the man on the other side, "What is it, Olaf?" The burly warrior took a step back, instinctively setting off Fallon's uncanny abilities to detect certain amiss. There was a peculiar air of unease about the man and a particular glint of fear in his eyes. This took Fallon unaware for the bearded warrior was not accustomed to showing his weakness, especially to him.

He thrived off instinct and in that moment, he felt something was terribly underway. He knew not whether to contribute the slight inkling to his warrior-like senses or to sheer luck, either way, he knew to heed them well.

The corridor was eerily dark and unnaturally stilled.

The keep was far too quiet for his liking.

He cast shrewd, golden eyes upon his brother's man. Olaf was a brute-sort, not easily shaken or deterred by any man, but Fallon was keen to note the certain shade of pallor that colored his face, a slight dampening of sweat bathed the perimeter of his brow betraying his apprehension.

Fallon narrowed a cutting glare on the man-he had never truly trusted him, nor had he ever been given a reason too.

"I wish to speak with you of a certain matter, milord."

He was taken aback by the anxiousness in Olaf's voice. Though the hall was almost pitch-black, he thought he noticed the man's face go a little paler, draining his staunch expression entirely of any color. "What matter?"

Olaf fell silent-the anxiety in the air heightening to an almost smothering degree.

"It concerns the incident shortly after the attack on Godwinson."

Fallon froze; a sudden daunting chill snaked down his spine, turning the blood in his veins ice cold.

The particular incident Olaf referred too could only be the one fatal happening he had pushed to the dark recesses of his mind; one that had nearly cost him his life. The day he was attacked by a faceless army whom he had never sought to right his anger.

A poisonous notion fleetingly passed through him, but he refused to acknowledge it, he couldn't, the thought of it was almost inconceivable.

"What about it?" the question was released on a nasty growl. He hadn't realized he had spoken it aloud, until the stout warrior flinched from his rough baritone.

An uncertain play of emotions shifted Olaf's expression. The warrior struggled to reveal what would surely be his undoing.

"Speak, man!" his voice had arisen to a fierce-pitch, the sound resounding like thunder within the hall.

"You were betrayed, milord-" Olaf spieled, "You weren't attacked by the Saxons."

He shook his head in disbelief, "I was attacked by Harold's men-"

"Nay, my liege-" Olaf interjected, "It was merely set in that manner so that you would believe 'twas Harold's men."

Olaf's words somewhat fell on deaf ears. Fallon struggled against the rushing, vivid pain of that day-the kick delivered to his face and ribs, the distinct, ominous sound of laughter, men laughing at his expanse. How could he forget the ultimate blow that had stolen the breath from him-the dagger plunged mercilessly into his chest?

He couldn't fathom the indication in Olaf's rising confession and yet, the truth of it glinted fearfully in the man's eyes.

A violent rage flowed through him, like a rapid river, growing fierce in its course. A red haze invaded his vision, a fury building, brimming beneath the surface as something to the effect of adamant rage settled like stone. He figured his half-brother capable of cruelty and other means of bitter tendencies, but to think him prone to committing murder of his own kin?

He should have detected Curran's hatred for him long ago-it had been here all along, yet he had failed to notice it, and that fatal error had nearly killed him.

Death nearly delivered at the hands of his brother?

Curran had betrayed him-his own flesh and blood.

The redness in his eyes dissipated long enough for him to level a cold, menacing glare on Olaf. He could so easily snap the man's neck if he deemed it, instead, he grasped onto some semblance of sanity before giving into the stark madness that consumed him.

"Curran devised the plan long before the attack on Harold. He believed no one would question your death at Hastings-he planned to peg your fall on the enemy."

The muscle at his jaw twitched as he stepped toward Olaf. The stout warrior tensed, expecting a blow, or worse, a blade.

Fallon peered down at the man and said quite calmly, "Count your blessings, old man, for if it not for your loose tongue; I would have killed you without respite."

He wasn't certain, but he thought a shudder of relief passed through the ample warrior but he caught a lingering glint of fear in his open stare.

And then, struck with a sudden notion, he felt compelled to ask- "Why would you risk telling me this?"

Olaf straightened, "My loyalty no longer lies with your brother-his infatuation with that woman-"

Something propelled him forward, whether it be another foreboding instinct, or sheer alarm, he slammed Olaf against the opposing wall, pinning the warrior with his forearm jammed against his throat, cutting off any other words that may have spilled forth. "Where is my brother now?" he demanded, a fleeting fear passing through him.

Olaf spat a few incoherent replies but Fallon was beyond listening. He wrenched away and half-ran down the corridor-a terrible panic gripping him unlike anything he'd ever encountered, even in the throes of battle, forcing his heart in a rage, but he knew, even as he jerked her door open and moved to her bed, that she was long gone.

The rope that bounded her wrists was beginning to chafe her skin raw. No matter how much she tugged and pulled, her restraints remained firm. She felt tears of frustration along with a mingling of fear choke her.

Instead of giving into the natural urge to cry, she straightened her spine and glared heatedly into the back of her captor.

She wouldn't give him the satisfaction of seeing her cry, but it was proving difficult to stay resilient when thoughts of possibly never seeing Fallon again flooded her mind.

How could she have been so foolish? She should have confessed her feelings-she loved him, hopelessly and most beguilingly. Her heart yearned for Fallon; craved his love unlike anything she'd ever felt. She'd risk all the dangers in the world to have his undying love. She had been afraid and now in this particular moment, she couldn't quite pin-point her reasons for being so frightened, and now, she may never be given another chance to tell him exactly how she felt.

That disheartening thought brought another swarm of un-shed tears.

"Sniveling doesn't suit you."

Her spine went rigid as her eyes connected roughly with that cold-wolfish glare.

They had stopped briefly to rest and it was the first time Curran had spoken since abducting her from her chamber.

He stood by their horse, studying her with a look that chilled as well as enraged her. If not for the cloth jammed uncomfortably in her mouth, she would have told him to go to hell-by the sudden awry glint in his eyes, she detected he guessed at her thoughts.

His mouth curled into a grin, "That's more like it."

He moved toward her and she tensed, watching him un-easily as he knelt down where she sat and reached out to yank the cloth from her mouth. "Have you something to spout from that pretty mouth?"   Her eyes glinted daggers as she swallowed to alleviate some of the dryness in her throat. "Bastard." She rasped.

His grin widened, "Aye that I am."

"Why are you doing this?" she demanded, "Do you wish to provoke William?"

His silver eyes hardened, "On the contrary, I seek to gain my King's approval." He paused, his eyes moving slowly over her, "It is Fallon I wish to break."

She frowned, "Why, he is your brother-"

"Half-" he snapped, "surely you would have guessed it all by now, sweet?" he reached out and seized her arm, wincing beneath the pressure of his fingers. "I am the illegitimate son of Alaric Macaulay-born from a woman whose purpose in life was to please my father's lustful needs; a mere serving wench, a lowly peasant woman so unlike the lovely Lady Jocelyn with her golden hair who produced Alaric a son, the only son to inherit all of which my father possessed." His expression turned grim, "And what of the son produced by a mere thrall? What was to become of an illegitimate boy?"

Alana attempted to pry herself free of the grip that tightened ever so painfully with each of Curran's angry words.

"I have desired nothing more than to have all of which my brother claims-and now our King shows my brother favoritism, just as my father had done. I thought mayhap if I killed Fallon myself, I could easily assert my position at Linden, regain a title stolen from me, and maybe even gain William's favor."

Alana gasped, horrified as she recalled that altering day when she had come upon Fallon, at death's door, in the forest. "You were responsible for what happened to Fallon?" a sob lodged tightly in her throat, her chest tightening with a terrible ache at what Fallon would feel once he learned this horrifying truth.

She felt a sickening feeling when a smile curved Curran's lips, his eyes lacking any trace of regret. "It would have worked so masterfully, as I had originally planned-who could have possibly guessed that the 'Fury's' own brother would devise his downfall?" his ominous grin faded, "But that all changed the second you came strolling down that path."

He reached out and she pulled away but his fingers seized her chin cruelly gripping her face, "You shouldn't meddle in others affairs-but then, I suppose if you hadn't, I wouldn't have you now." His silver eyes shifted to a piercing gray and for a second, Alana thought she captured fleeting warmth as his gaze lingered mindfully on her and very quietly he added, "You are the only woman to penetrate my brother's heart-and now I've claimed even that."

Disgusted, she wrenched out of his hand and brought her wrists in full-circle, slamming them against his smirking face.

When he toppled sideways, she lunged to her feet and began in a mindless run around the boulder and directly into the path of a mass swarm of men and horses.

Chapter 36

Alana's chest swelled with relief at the sight that approached her, her joy at seeing Alec McLeod so overwhelming that at first, she hadn't noticed their battle attire. He would see her back to Linden.

Nudging his horse forward, Alec accessed her from the saddle. "Have you lost your way, milady?"

Alana's relief turned to dread as her eyes swept the heavily armored men. She took a step back, averting her eyes back to Alec. "What goes here?" she asked tentatively.

A voice behind her spoke garishly, "Aye McLeod, tell the lass what you have planned this day."

Alana stiffened as a hand gripped her elbow and she was more alarmed by the steel blade extended from Curran's other hand, pointed directly at McLeod.

Alec turned his gaze upon Curran and grinned, "You plan to wield a blade against my forces, Macaulay, you alone?" his sloe-eyes wavered to Alana, "Or does the lass have a dirk up her skirts?"

Alana's face flushed angrily-she had once thought this man kind. Her eyes glanced at the men to Alec's back, one slight man in particular garbed in a cloak from head to toe. She felt a fear hasten through her-surely Curran didn't think he could best all these men on his own?

The blade that hovered between them and Alec not once swayed.

"I was told the 'Fury' was a man of his word-" Alec spoke firstly, his dark eyes glinting harshly, "-a man known for his supposed word has broken his treaty with my father and with that-has produced an enemy of us."

Cold, silver eyes narrowed intensely on McLeod, "You didn't come on behalf of your father-you came for the King. You think I don't know of your treason, your plans to assassinate William? I was on to you before the troth was arranged."

Alec's jaw tightened, "You have no proof of this."

Curran snickered, "One can learn a lot from raiding-villages will talk. Your sister's betrothal to my brother worked in your favor-always aware of the King's whereabouts."

Alec straightened in his saddle grinning as he motioned to the grim faces behind him. "Do you plan to kill all of us, Macaulay, how unfortunate for you that my men and I happened to cross your path."

Curran's grin widened, "You fail to notice, McLeod, I purposely walked this path."

Alec stiffened in the saddle as the surrounding thickets rustled, the greenery shifting as men from all angles stepped into the clearing, each raising a blade as equally menacing as the one Curran maneuvered.

Ambush.

Alec's men produced their swords, the air filling with a tension as thick as blood.

Alana's stomach clenched with alarm.

"The odds are looking better." Curran said smugly.

"Indeed." Alec chimed throwing one leg over the saddle and jumping to the earth. He pulled his sword from his scabbard and stepped toward Curran, raising it defensively. "Any man can wield a blade, but can he do so skillfully?"

It erupted so abruptly, the sudden clashing of steel against steel broke out in flurry of madness.

Alana felt a hand at her back, pushing her from harms way.

The second she hit the ground, she rolled away from the impending fall of feet that threatened to stomp her as blades struck above her.

Once upright, she began to tug and pull on her wrists, the rope cutting into her flesh but she was mindless to the pain and very much aware of the certain peril surrounding her.

She stole a glance towards Curran but something moving toward her in her peripheral drew her attention.

She froze as the cloaked-man she had noticed earlier moved toward her.

Her heart in her throat, she began yanking more earnestly at her bindings.

The man came to stand over her; Alana tensed as a frightened breath shuddered through her. The man reached up and pushed the hood away from his face.

Alana gasped as the sun revealed sleek, black hair and eyes as correspondingly dark brimming with such malice.

"Rosalind-" Alana said sharply.

Rosalind grinned crookedly and slowly drew a dagger from the arm of her cloak. "I can kill you and Fallon will never know it was I that delivered it-with you dead, he'll come back to me."

Alana shook her head, taken aback by the crazed-cynical gleam to her eyes. "You're mad, Rosalind." Alana exclaimed, "When Fallon learns of Alec's treason, there's no hope for you."

Rosalind's face twisted grudgingly, "You bitch, if it weren't for you, everything would have gone accordingly!" with a cry, she lunged toward Alana, raising her dagger-

Alana tensed, planting her arms directly before her to take the blow, but the moment she anticipated the impact, Rosalind screamed, forcing Alana's eyes open.

Rosalind's sloe-eyes rounded with pain her face paling markedly from the arrow rooted firmly in her chest.

She released a guttural breath and then toppled to the ground.

Alana's head snapped around and followed the direction where the arrow had come. Her heart swelled at the sight of Nettie.

A sort of rage mingled with fear propelled him into the madness in the valley up ahead.

Fallon reached down and wrapped a steady hand around the hilt of his sword. He didn't have to look over his shoulder to know that his men trailed behind-even the damned cousin had followed, insisting that she would be of use. He had been skeptical up until the moment he saw Rosalind looming over Alana, lunging toward her with a dagger.

He had barely pulled his sword free of its scabbard before an arrow whisked fleetingly through the air, implanting itself gravely in Rosalind's chest.

He gave a slight pause to peer quickly over his shoulder at the man who brandished it, only to be utterly taken aback to see Alana's cousin lower her bow.

Making a mental note to later praise the usually skittish-prone woman, he dug his heels into his horse and propelled forward. The second he spotted Curran, he dropped from his horse, landing easily onto his hunches, arose and the instant he did, caught a blade hovering above him.

He felt the muscles in his forearm tense as the burly warrior that spurred toward him push Fallon's blade downward. Gritting his teeth, he dug his heels into the earth and with a sudden momentum, shoved the man backward.

The warrior stumbled allowing Fallon to seize the moment and deliver a fatal blow.

He spotted Alana and started toward her.

Alana's heart thrust violently against her chest at the sight of Fallon and his men; she was even more startled to see Nettie trailing closely at Gavin's side.

She struggled to her feet and peered despairingly down at Rosalind feeling a slight tinge of remorse for the woman.

She pulled at her bindings and cringed as the rope chafed a raw path in her skin.

"Alana-" Fallon's voice resounded through the unmistakable sound of men meeting their certain death, her chest swelled with relief and then sheer alarm as he fought his way through the armored men that charged him.

She spotted Ranulf's massive frame moving quickly up behind Fallon and taking out a man that would have surely severed Fallon in two.

Ivan's usually charismatic face was now pulled taut with an intenseness that altered his face completely and for the first time since meeting the man, Alana was mindful of the impeccable warrior he kept well concealed.

Gavin sheathed his sword and wielded it with an ease that came naturally to him. Alana was more in awe of the transformed woman that protected his back. Nettie had learned to master the bow and arrow at a tender age as she but had never truly taken to it-but as Alana watched her cousin, she managed it well, protecting Gavin with the utmost skill.

Fallon continued to fight his way toward her but a sudden thwarted cry rang from the massacre.

Somewhere in the midst of blades and armor, bloodshed and tears, a prominent figure hit the ground-

Alana felt a shudder in the core.

Curran lay dead.

Chapter 37

A ghastly sound expelled from somewhere and Fallon realized the awful cry spewed forth from his throat as his eyes fell on Curran's motionless body.

All the rage gathered within him, he spurred forward, heedless to the blades that whizzed by him. If a sword had struck him, he wouldn't have felt it in that blind haze as a fire propelled him towards McLeod.

He channeled all his fury into his arm as Alec turned widely about to intercept his powerful blow.

McLeod's arm trembled beneath the impact, his knees buckling beneath the imminent force of Fallon's blade.

"Where is your King now?" Alec taunted, his grip tightening around the hilt of his sword though he struggled against the blade that hovered above his face.

Gold eyes burned precariously back at him, "I don't need my King to kill you."

Fallon reacted, rearing back to bring his heel upward to connect promptly with McLeod's midriff. The sudden maneuver sent Alec sprawled to the ground, landing roughly on his back.

Fallon stepped forward and raised his blade-

A small hand gripped his arm, forcing him still. Fallon turned and all the rage in him filtered away at Alana's lovely face. "Don't kill him, Fallon." Unshed tears shimmered in her sea-green eyes, "Let William decide his fate."

He stared into her beautiful face and there saw his own pain mirrored. He reached up and gently cupped her cheek.

The abrupt sound of horses approaching stirred his attention. Fallon lifted his head and saw William coming down the hill, his men following closely behind.

He leveled a cold glare on McLeod, "I may have spared your life but my King will not be so merciful."

Fallon stepped away and Ranulf and Ivan moved forward to seize Alec. He turned and crossed to where Curran lay unmoving.

He plunged his sword into the earth and knelt down beside him. A tightness squeezed his chest and a wrenching tore at his gut as he stared gravely at his brother.

He tilted his head to shield his pain as a shudder gripped him.

"Fallon-" a pained, hollow voice brought his head upright.

"Curran." He breathed incredulously.

A deathly pallor washed over him, his eyes more silver than they've ever appeared; a slight faraway glint overtaking their vividness. "I h-have wronged you." Every word came out on a shallow breath.

Fallon winced inwardly, "Nay, brother."

Curran swallowed, the small movement causing him great discomfort. "Aye, I tried to kill y-you."

"I'm hard to kill." Fallon teased, though his heart twisted with grief.

Curran attempted to shake his head but the pain forced him still.

Fallon inhaled a deep, unsteady breath. "All is forgiven." He exclaimed truthfully.

Silver eyes glistened tearfully, "I am not deserving of your f-forgiveness."

A shadow fell over them but Fallon kept his eyes locked on his brother. A gentle touch smoothed over his arm as Alana settled beside him.

Curran's eyes flickered toward Alana, "F-forgive me."

Alana forced a timid smile and reached out to gently clasp his hand in her own. His fingers tightened weakly around hers and then loosened.

She felt Fallon's body stiffen as the light in Curran's eyes ebbed, dying away with his last breath.

Clenching his jaw, Fallon arose and turned to peer intensely at McLeod who was being led away by William's men.

"You did well, 'Fury'."

Fallon stiffened as William approached, his stern voice carried easily in the sudden, restless wind.

"Thank you, my liege." He replied grudgingly, casting a lingering look on Curran.

William's dark eyes followed Fallon's desolate gaze, "Your brother shall have a proper burial."

Fallon could only nod, the ache in his chest growing.

William stepped forward and laid a hand to Fallon's shoulder, drawing his attention. "If not for your brother, we may have learned of McLeod's uprising too late and suffered a grander fatality."

Fallon remained silent, the hollowness in his chest growing almost intolerable.

The valley was cleared of fallen bodies, both enemy and ally combined. McLeod and his treacherous followers were immediately shackled and now well on there way to Lincoln, William eager to make an example of them.

Fallon had sought his only means of comfort-mead.

He sat in the dismal, darkened hall and stared bleakly at the grand doors expecting his wry-laced brother to coming strolling through them at any moment.

He took a long swig from his canter and slammed it onto the table.

Damn you, Curran.

Finding no solace in his cup, he tossed it across the room and swiveled from his chair, turning to brace his weight against the stone wall.

Absorbed in his anger and conflictions he hadn't heard the doors open until a gentle voice called to him.

"Fallon."

His chest tightened at Alana's sweet voice.

"Leave me." He growled; he could barely brace the pain on his own, let alone with another soul.

When a stretch of silence followed, he thought she had hastened from the room until a tender touch smoothed over his back.

The muscles there jolted at the unexpected gentleness and not thinking, he spun around and seized her wrists unmercifully. "Don't!"

He caught the wince that pinched her face even as her green eyes widened from the tempest that burned in his eyes.

Puzzled by her flinch of pain, he peered down where his hands latched around her wrists and loosened his hold turning them over to inspect-his stomach churned at the sight-the skin of her delicate wrists were torn and raw, reddened from the rope that had earlier secured them.

He dropped her wrists as if they had burned to the touch and stepped away from her. "Leave me be, Alana."

Alana stiffened, somewhat hurt by his rejection of her, but she was determined not to be frightened away-he was hurting, far more than she.

She stared at his stiff back, amazed that he could contain his pain so tightly.

She peered down at her wrists-she had yet to care for them, she had thought of nothing other than Fallon since returning to Linden, even tending to her slight wounds appeared petty in that moment.

Summoning her muster, she raised her chin and gazed intently upon his back. "I will not let you frighten me away." She breathed in a breath when he turned to peer at her, "Everyone else may fear you, but I do not."

The tempest she had recognized a moment ago returned full-blazed as he took a step toward her. "You tread dangerous ground, Alana." His voice had deepened, revealing somewhat of a feeble restraint for whatever storm lay dormant.

Her breaths came faster, "You do not scare me."

Although she stood her ground, her legs began to tremble as he closed the space between them, suddenly looming above her, his massive chest mere inches from her own.

His amber eyes blazed with an insatiable flame and she knew not what emotions fed that searing. "I warn you for the last time-" she trembled at the anger hinted in his tone, "-leave me now."

Her body shuddered but she did no more than lift her chin, her eyes challenging.

His massive chest rose and fell with a deep breath and she was aware of a heat emanating from his body, wrapping her in a sensual cocoon. She should have been frightened; she should have heeded his warning.

His arm lashed out, seized her roughly around the waist and jerked her flush against him. The second her body connected hotly with his rigid frame, a gasp erupted from her lips soon muffled by the slam of his mouth upon hers.

The intensity of his kiss startled a tiny cry from her but he silenced it by deepening his ardor, pressing his mouth possessively into the sweetness of her own, delving his tongue swiftly within.

Alana gave a startled cry as he swept her off her feet, his hands splaying her firm bottom, pressing her hard against his swollen passion.

A fire erupted from somewhere in her loins as he plunged his tongue deeper, teasing her lower lip and pulling delectably at her mouth.

He stepped a few strides and she felt him lowering her to the table, laying her gently on her back.

She gave a soft cry when the kiss ended abruptly but gave a sharp gasp when he tugged her forward, pushed her thighs apart and stepped between them.

He reached up and pulled out what little restraint held her glorious mane of red hair and splayed his fingers through the length of it. His fingers kneaded softly through her tresses, pulling and tugging lightly, tilting her head back to claim her mouth fervently.

"So beautiful-" he breathed against her throat, pressing his lips against the ardent pulse that throbbed there.

His arm wrapped around her waist, pulling her earnestly up against him as he trailed hot kisses down the length of her throat, along her collar-bone and down into the valley of her breasts.

Alana's skin tingled with every electrifying kiss, every intensified caress-her hands mingled in the tunic that clung to his chest and she had the demanding urge to rip it from him, revealing the rippling muscle beneath.

A shock resonated through her when his hand dipped low to cup her breast.

"Fallon-" she said in a mindless, fervent haze.

She felt his hair tickle her chest as he shook his head, grinning into her throat as he whispered heatedly. "No escaping now, my fiery love."

Chapter 38

There was an edge to his voice that gave her pause and when peering into his amber eyes she was taken aback by the woefulness reflected there. Her heart wrenched with empathy for within his eyes she witnessed not a hardened warrior, but a man abundant with great pain.

She felt tears at the back of her eyes as an understanding dawned. He leaned forward and rested his head against her breast, and she held him, wrapping her arms around his massive frame. She ran her hands the length of his back, teasing the strands that rested amongst his shoulders, all the while, being that leverage, willing to take the weight of all his agonies.

Outside this room, he was a fearsome, sword-wielding warrior, but here, within her arms, she found a tormented man.

He lifted his head and eyes stormy with afflictions gazed deeply into hers. He reared up and claimed her lips. She opened her mouth to him and his tongue dipped inside, rolling and teasing. She felt his hastiness, his eagerness to claim her and when he pushed her skirts up, she shuddered with anticipation.

He was hurting and she gave no second thought to his claiming, his way of seizing something back. What fate is there for a warrior who's chosen a path certain of bloodshed and pain? If she could offer him a moments of happiness, a willingness to love unconditionally, she would give that, wholeheartedly. She would love him, now and forever.

He kissed her deeply, possessively, almost painfully, but she wasn't afraid. Her hands unraveled from his tunic, flattening to explore the solid chest beneath.

She whimpered in delight beneath his lavished kisses.

His hands roamed over her freely, exploring every luscious curve, implanting every intricate line that made up her delectable body infinitely in his mind.

He bent her over his arm, pressing heated, hungry kisses to the lively pulse quivering beneath his mouth.

"So beautiful-" he whispered hoarsely as he nuzzled the hollow at the base of her throat.

His hand moved to the front of his breeches where the evidence of his arousal bulged eagerly. Her heart jolted heatedly as he undid the front and his manhood came free.

His hand moved to the nape of her neck as he hungrily kissed her, pressing hot, ardent kisses to her lips, chin and jaw.

He stepped further into the cradle of her thighs and grabbing her waist, jerked her closer, tighter against him. She arched into his chest as he fastened his lips to the pulse beating feverishly there.

"Alana-" he groaned tensely.

Her eyes fluttered closed, breathless and utterly pliant, she melted in his arms. The jolt of pain as he entered her came unexpectedly and she cried out with it. He recaptured her lips, muffling her cry and cupped her cheek gently.

He paused, giving her body a moment to adjust to the massive size of him and than slowly he began to move. The pain she felt started to fade, and with that, followed promptly, a kindling flame, slowly streaming like hot liquid. She cried out as he thrust into her, and again, producing a maddening hunger as he stroked her gently, kissing her lovingly with unbridled passion. She shuddered breathlessly as she met each thrust, moving with him and when he gave a cry of his own, a white-hot flame obscured everything, and all stood still but their lovemaking.

Her heart pounding, she lay unmoving with her arms wrapped lovingly around him. He didn't move he remained with their bodies joined with his head against her breast and for a time they remained as so.

She had never felt such overwhelming feelings-she couldn't describe it, but all she knew was that her heart was going to explode. She wanted him with every fiber in her being, in every way imaginable. Her heart swelled with her fierce realization. She loved him. She loved Fallon.

Before she could stop herself, the words spewed forth from her lips, "I love you, Fallon." She declared gently.

She felt him stiffen in her arms and then he pulled away with a sudden draft. Her eyes grew round as she watched him adjust his breeches and then sweep an unsteady hand through his tousled hair.

Her heart began to pace profoundly in her chest, for those words she had spoken so passionately, so sincerely a moment ago, now hung uneasily in the air.

She noticed the tension in his jaw, the rigidness of his frame as he turned to her, his sunlit eyes foreshadowed with gloom, "You don't love me, Alana." He said grimly.

She didn't know which hurt more, his disregard of her acclaimed love, or his words spoken so coldly, like a dagger to her heart; most of all, the final blow, his heedlessness to express his love. Doubt began to take root-did he even love her?

Dropping her head she shakily adjusted her skirts and gathered to her feet. Resisting tears the sting of tears and fighting the quivering of her chin, she raised her head and met his hardened eyes, "You cannot tell me what I feel. You push everyone away, even your own feelings. You're so bull-headed you can't even recognize love when it's right in your face. You're a coward, Fallon "The Fury"."

Gathering her skirts, she moved toward the door, her body rigid, her eyes burning with unshed tears, she felt his eyes at her back. She waited until she entered the corridor and then she began to sob.

Later that evening, the men rejoiced in the hall, supping mead and nursing minor cuts and abrasions. Alana mustered her pride and joined them, only to find Fallon missing amongst the men. She felt a blush creep up her neck to redden her cheeks as she recalled their lovemaking.

Dismissing the notion to avoid the sudden pang of hurt that came regardless, she moved about the room to see to the warriors.

Ivan was the first to grace her with a cheeky grin, "Milady." He said charmingly, "How do you fare?"

She smiled, "Well Ivan, you?"

He banged a balled fist against his hard chest, "I'm invincible, milady."

"Balderdash!" Ranulf exclaimed in a beastly manner, "You're just a lucky son-a-bitch."

Alana was startled for the giant warrior rarely expressed humor and was taken aback by the sarcasm laced in his baritone.

Ivan chuckled, "Aye, mayhap, but I am exceptionally swift, a remarkable ability that keeps me unscathed, unlike you my surly friend, who moves with the grace of a burly bear."

A hint of a grin pulled at Ranulf's scarred mouth.

Alana noticed than a deep gash along the warrior's beefy arm. She crossed the room to him and their eyes met. "You are hurt." She affirmed.

"I have fared worse, milady."

It was the first time he had addressed her so kindly, "May I put salve on it to keep it from festering?"

At first, he appeared as though he would object and then he nodded grudgingly. She smiled and turned to retrieve her medicines. She noticed than that Gavin and Nettie would no where to be seen.

Lynette moved through the corridors seeking her cousin. The earlier happenings of the day had taken a toll on her and she was eager for a remedy that would chase the throbbing from her head. So absorbed with her notions, she rounded the corner and collided into a sinewy frame. Strong, assured hands reached up to steady her and when she raised her head, her eyes connected with a pair of warm, hazel eyes.

Gasping, she took a step back and than collecting her composure, raised her chin and said haughtily, "Gavin."

A devilish grin pulled at his fine mouth, "Lynette."

Her name on his lips produced a tingling along her skin, "Something I can do for you, Norman?" she demanded with emphasis.

His grin broadened as his eyes moved appreciatively over her face, "I seek your company."

Her brow arched, "Why not seek your Norman friends out?"

He crossed his arms against his muscled chest, "Their currently entertaining their thirst, and I have a hankering for something other than drink."

Her eyes narrowed heatedly, "Appease your thirst elsewhere." She started around him but yelped when his hand stopped her.

She raised her eyes to his and was startled by the softening of his warrior face, "I have no intention of hurting you, Lynette. You compare me to a tragedy and I am sorry this has happened to you, give me a chance to show you that I am unlike your supposed demons."

She remained silent, peering deeply into those meaningful hazel eyes. When they had battled alongside each other earlier that day, it had felt rightfully so, as though standing at this man's side was what fate had intended.

His hand fell away from her arm and he reached up to gently cup her chin, "If you let me, I wish to protect you, assuage your sorrows, and love you always, forever."

Her heart jolted with the promise laced in his velvety tone and when he pulled her into his arms, she didn't object but rather delved delightedly in it.

So much has occurred she couldn't wrap her senses around it; Curran's death and his disclosed attempt to kill Fallon. She couldn't imagine how Fallon must be feeling about his brother's deception and loss; and McLeod's treason against the King. She needed solace, she needed an escape. She thought of her village and her beloved neighbors whom she'd abandoned and felt a pang of guilt. She thought of sweet old Agatha who'd lost her husband, and Rowan who'd given his life for his fellow villagers. How could she have forgotten them?

She would find them and make amends for her abandonment. She would rebuild the village, no matter the obstacles that stood in her way, she'd start anew, begin another life. The next morning, when she revealed her plans to Nettie, she was startled when her beloved cousin expressed her desire to stay at Linden Keep.

"I have no desire to part from you, dear cousin. Please stay with me." Nettie cried softly, tears dotting her cheekbones.

Alana clasped her cousin's hands in her own, "Nor do I, more sister than cousin, but I need to ensure that our people are safe."

Nettie's blue eyes welled with tears, "You will return, aye?"

Alana felt her mouth flatten grimly-she wasn't so sure she'd plan on returning but nodded to appease her cousin.

They hugged tightly and kissed one another's brow.

Alana bid the warriors a farewell, taking notice that Fallon was vacant from the hall. Ivan, in his own humorous way, pleaded for her to stay. Gavin charmingly planted a kiss on her hand, all the while, holding Nettie lovingly beneath his arm. Ranulf, giant and scarred, stood away from them, watching with a knowing expression. They merely exchanged glances and naught more was said.

As Alana made her way from the keep she paused, heart pounding, she wanted desperately to see Fallon once more before her departure, but decided against it. She had confessed her love to him and he'd shunned it. She wasn't so certain she could face him without succumbing to tears.

Donning a cloak, she stepped out into the morning light. With the sun high in the sky and a distant breeze trailing the highlands, all appeared seemingly well. She had a long way to go, but she was certain she remembered the way and with her bow and arrows, she wasn't unprotected.

A horse was saddled and brought to her and as she mounted, she cast a longing glance toward the keep.

As she turned her head away, someone called forcibly, "Alana!"

Her hands froze around the reins, her heart jolted against her breast as she turned her head around.

Fallon appeared from the mouth's keep, running toward her, golden hair glistening beneath the early sun. His eyes, as amber as ever, impelled her angrily.

"Where do you think you're going?" he demanded crossly as he came to stand before her mare.

She felt her own anger rise, "I don't believe that is any of your concern."

His jaw flexed and his eyes flared bright, "You are my concern." She had little time to react as he stepped forward, grabbed a hold of her cloak and jerked her down. She fell clumsily into his arms and with that began to struggle.

He turned and started back to the keep only to stop at her sharp command, "Put me down!"

He set her on her feet, "You call me the coward, but I find this-" he swept a hand to the horse behind him, "-you, running away?"

Her face flared red, "I wasn't running; my people need me."

His nostrils widened with an inhaled breath, "I need you, Alana."

She blanched and within her chest her heart swelled with hopefulness.

She stared up at him, searching the depths of his amber eyes to see her love reflected but something beyond his shoulder caught her attention, a shadow, moving abruptly toward them. As it came fast, her eyes widened with profound alarm and she reacted instantaneously, moving to plant her body between Fallon's back and the man barreling toward them with a fiery, vengeful gaze and a menacing fire that propelled his blade.

Chapter 39

When he came too, he found himself dispersed among a bed with a throbbing temple. He pushed up and was stayed by a sturdy hand.

"Easy, my liege." Ranulf assuaged, his scarred face set in grimness.

Fallon blinked to awareness just as a tightness gripped his chest, "Alana?"

The big warrior said nothing, propelling Fallon from the bed. He swayed on his feet but regained his stance, moving hastily towards the door. The burly warrior moved quickly, implanting himself in his path.

"Move." Fallon growled ominously, amber eyes burning.

"You nearly killed McLeod with your hands-"

"He is not dead?"

Ranulf shook his head, "We've detained him."

Fallon's jaw tightened, "Not for long."

He took a step forward and Ranulf put a hand to his chest, "My liege, now is not time for vengeance."

Fallon inhaled a deep, unsteady breath and then asked dauntingly, "Is it grave?"

A flickering of unease glinted warily in the warrior's dark eyes, "The severity of her wound we know not."

Fallon pushed by the burly warrior and started for her chambers. When he stepped into the room, the sight that greeted him brought him dead in his strides.

She lay motionless, her lips lacking their dusty shade of pink, her cheeks without their rosy hue; the sickly pallor of her skin bathed in perspiration declared the graveness of her wound. Even the loveliness of her glorious, red hair dimmed in radiance. Her clothes had been carefully removed and just beneath the edge of the coverlet, he could see the bandaging soaked with blood.

Nettie sobbed softly at her side, her face streaked in tears and heavy with heart. Ivan stood like a shadow in the corner, his long, solemn face etched severely with concern and next to him, Gavin, stood erect, his face tightly drawn with evident dismay.

"Alana?" the hollowness in his voice matched the ache in his heart.

Ivan and Gavin straightened from the wall. Nettie hadn't turned around but remained weeping, clutching Alana's hand.

"Do something." He growled brokenly, to no one in particular, his eyes wild, teary. When silence answered his plea, he stalked to Nettie's side, "You will fix this!" he cried hoarsely.

Nettie winced beneath the fierceness in his tone, "I have not the skill as do Alana, I can only do what little was taught unto me." She answered painfully.

His hand lashed out and gripped her shoulder, "Nay-"

"Fallon!" Gavin fell in at his side and seized the hand curled around Nettie's shoulder, "Release her, my liege." He said respectfully, but the command was unmistakable.

Fallon rounded on him, seizing the warrior roughly about the tunic and shoving him forcibly against the wall. Ivan moved forward and pried a muscled arm back as Ranulf restrained the other jammed against Gavin's throat.

"She cannot die!"

He gathered all his fury and threw the men off his arms. He spun widely about and stormed from the room. His fierce, reddened path drove him to a darkened cell where McLeod's slumped frame lay sprawled on the dirtied floor.

He struck the door open with such violence it cracked soundly against the opposing wall, startling the bloodied man form his pained state, and as the light struck the man's badly swollen face, Fallon froze.

"Come to finish me off-" though his face was unrecognizable, the voice thickly laced with pain was unmistakably certain. Blood gurgled up from the man's throat and he rolled to his side and spat.

The rage that hummed through his body began to dissipate, "You fell a woman with your blade -" He said menacingly, "-you will die."

The man beneath the battered visage attempted a grin, "It would seem only fair-" he paused with strain, "-your woman for my daughter."

Fallon's jaw tensed, "Rosalind knew the risks when she entered the field. The blame rests with her."

He was startled by the tears that merged with the pain in McLeod's eyes, "My daughter is dead, and now you will know how it feels."

Feeling his rage return altogether, Fallon stepped further into the cell and leveled a cold, meaningful glare on the man, "If she dies, you die."

She awoke to pain, but was mindful to the steady breathing that passed through her lungs. She was alive and her last thought-a man barreling upon her with a blade aimed for her heart. She moaned as she reached up to run her hands the length of her chest. Her fingers smoothed over the bandaging there and she breathed in a painful breath.

She then heard an audible gasp and suddenly Nettie was at her side, "Alana, I've feared the worst."

Alana peered into her cousin's teary, blue eyes, "My wound?"

"I cleansed and sutured it, just as you taught me. I applied yarrow and myrrh. You've lost some blood, but no fatal blood vessels were severed. You will have a scar." She said this lastly with a dipped lilt.

Alana managed a weak smile, "If a scar is all I am to suffer, then I shall gladly wear it." She reached a hand out to Nettie, "You've done well." And then, as her mind came aware, her eyes widened, "Fallon?"

Nettie squeezed her hand assuredly, "He's alive because of you-"

"Alana."

Her heart swelled within her chest as her eyes drew to the man looming in the door. The grief anchored in those gold eyes struck her squarely in the chest and she forced a breath from her lungs.

She was vaguely aware that Nettie had left as she focused intently on Fallon. He crossed to her side and gathered her hand into his.

She studied his face-it appeared to have aged, wrecked with torment.

His eyes fastened earnestly on her face, "Are you in pain?"

She smiled, "Not much."

He dipped his golden head, shielding his eyes from hers, "Alana, I was so scared that I had lost you."

Her heart skipped a beat.

He lifted his head and their eyes connected, "Can you forgive me?"

Her eyes softened, "Fallon-"

"You are a woman of worth-" he reached out and gently cupped her cheek, "-you are my match in every way."

She felt tears gathering at the back of her eyes as they moved lovingly over his face.

"I love you, Alana. I have from the moment I set eyes on you. Without you, life is meaningless." He brought her hand to his lips and pressed a gentle kiss to her palm, "I would have you, forever, if you still want me?"

Tears caught on her lashes as she blinked, a smile broadening her lips as she squeezed his hand tightly, "I want you, my golden Norman."

His mouth stretched into an elated smile and he leaned forward to kiss her tenderly on the lips, "Then you'll marry me?" he whispered to her ear.

She gasped as he sat back to gaze at her and she was overcome with great mirth, "Aye!" she exclaimed wholeheartedly, tears starting anew.

And he mirrored her joy, clutching her face tenderly between his hands and kissing her with all the love in his heart.

Epilogue

She was Lady Macaulay-wife to the Fallon 'The Fury'. She felt that dull ache within her chest, reminding her all too well of a certain McLeod blade but the daunting notion brought naught but comfort. McLeod was a threat no more.

Her smile broadened as she smoothed a hand over her budding belly to the nestled babe within. Her eyes rose to the cerulean sky and watched as white clouds drifted lazily by and she would forever remember the day that narrowing path brought her Norman to her.

"Alana!" she resisted a grin as Nettie came running, her voice strained with disapproval. "What are you doing?" she demanded once she reached Alana.

Alana's eyes swept Linden countryside and all its inhabitants working tediously in rebuilding the village. There was naught on this day that could keep her at bay, even her sweet cousin's bantering.

Her smile widened as her eyes swept the many faces around her. Her father would be proud. She had done her people by right. She spied sweet, old Agatha passing pitchers of water to the many laborers straining vigorously beneath the afternoon sun, among these laborers she spied Ivan winking playfully at the lass Kinsley as she passed him with a softening stare, whilst Gavin fell in at his side, nudging his beguiled friend jerkily with a hint of a grin before finding Nettie with all the love in his eyes.

Her gaze traveled further until finding the imposing stance of Ranulf. He moved about in his usual loner manner, moving timber too and from.

It was than that Alana spied the child, Kinsley's wee sister, hastening to catch up with the other children.

The little girl took a hard fall, landing roughly to her knees. Alana stiffened, prepared to aid the small child but was taken aback and stilled with awe as the scarred warrior knelt before the teary child. Alana watched in wonder as the big warrior, appearing massive aside the little girl, gently whispered words of something soothing to ease the child's hurt. The child smiled despite her pain and Ranulf righted her easily to her feet before playfully tapping the bridge of her nose. The tiny girl, undaunted by Ranulf's warrior face, giggled delightfully before fleeing in the direction of her playmates.

Alana continued to watch the scarred warrior as he gathered to his massive height, such an impeccable force, yet capable of easing a child's hurt.

They caught eyes and after a moment, he tilted his head with a silent smile before returning to his labor.

"Alana-" Nettie interjected her musings, "-have you a care for the babe?" she demanded.

"I cannot abide my stifling chambers a moment longer."

Her eyes alight with mirth moved continuously over the many faces until settling on one golden head in particular working mercifully alongside his warriors.

Her husband.

As if aware of her gaze, Fallon straightened and turned. His amber eyes flared with an anger all his own.

His jaw rigid, he began to stalk toward her.

"You see-" Nettie exclaimed.

Once Fallon reached her side, looming above her in all his golden swarthy, she could do no more than grin.

"Damnation woman you'll be the death of me." He said this sternly with an undertone of gingerly softness.

"I haven't done aught." She said innocently, smiling sweetly up at him.

He raised a golden brow and she detected a shadow of a grin, "You haven't done aught? You should be abed, not wandering the countryside in this blistering heat!"

Her eyes left his momentarily to survey the village. "They will be happy here." Her eyes grew teary and her heart swelled with an overwhelming joy that couldn't be expressed in words.

Fallon reached out and cupped her chin gently, turning her gaze back to him. "You are happy than, my wife?"

She smiled, "Aye, very much."

He grinned, "Than the world is at peace."

She giggled as he swept a muscled arm about her waist, reeling her tenderly against him, mindful of their babe resting comfortably between them.

He claimed her mouth passionately with all the love in his heart, holding on fiercely to his woman and child.

"My fiery Saxon, you, who stayed a blade for me, are my ever-beating heart." He whispered against her ear.

She met her husband's gentle, amber stare.

"As are you my golden Norman."

www.ingramcontent.com/pod-product-compliance
Lightning Source LLC
Chambersburg PA
CBHW071749190726
48292CB00003B/923